SHE HAD NEVER BEEN KISSED
LIKE THIS BEFORE . . .

Smooth, sensuous, his lips held her poised on the brink of an unknown pleasure. Her hands, pressed in restraint against his chest, lost their strength. She felt herself drawn closer and closer until her body seemed almost to merge with his, and still she was not close enough.

She knew it was all wrong, knew he could not be the man for her. But caught in his embrace, his kisses burning on her lips, she forgot all that, remembering only that he was the man she loved. . . .

More Romance from SIGNET

THE
ABDUCTED
HEART

by
Maxine Patrick

A SIGNET BOOK
NEW AMERICAN LIBRARY
TIMES MIRROR

COPYRIGHT © 1978 BY PATRICIA MAXWELL

SIGNET, SIGNET CLASSICS, MENTOR, PLUME AND MERIDIAN BOOKS
are published by The New American Library, Inc.,
1301 Avenue of the Americas, New York, New York 10019

FITST SIGNET PRINTING, JUNE, 1978

1 2 3 4 5 6 7 8 9

PRINTED IN THE UNITED STATES OF AMERICA

Chapter 1

It was going to be one of those days; Anne Matthews discovered that early. To begin with, she overslept. The small alarm clock that had been one of her presents when she left the family cottage of the Children's Home three years before had stopped during the night, ticking its last at half-past the witching hour. There was no time to sigh over it. She was late for work. Then in her haste to dress she snagged a run in her last pair of panty hose. A quick dab of clear nail polish prevented it from running further, and in any case it was hidden by the tongue of the sensible shoes she wore in her job as a caterer's assistant, but it left her feeling harried and unkempt. Neatness was important to her. There had been little of that commodity in the orphanage cottage shared with seven other foster brothers and sisters. Vaguely she could remember a quieter, more ordered time before her parents were killed when a bridge had collapsed, plunging their car into a flooded river in Louisiana. She could remember also the feeling of security she had known then, though she could not consciously bring to mind the faces of her parents or where and how they had lived. Still, those memories were enough to make her determined to use the secretarial skills she had been taught to reestablish that atmosphere around her. Toward that end, she adopted an air of calm efficiency. She wore

1

her shoulder-length hair in a smooth pageboy not because the style gave her hair the sheen of tawny silk, but because it was easy to keep under control. Because it saved time, she used the bare minimum of makeup, disregarding the dramatic potential of enormous eyes of a velvet brown softness fringed with thick, dark lashes. The clothes she bought herself were practical and easily cared for as became her no-nonsense image. It was not her fault that their severity did not suit the warm impulsiveness of her smile or the secretive, almost dreamy look that touched her delicate features in repose.

The morning did not improve once she left the small apartment she shared with a roommate, Judy Kramer. Judy, a secretary in a nice, dull office building nothing at all like Metcalf Caterers Inc., had the long weekend off. She had flown to New Orleans with her parents, leaving behind the small red Toyota, a present from her parents when she left home, for Anne to use. The only catch was that Judy had used it the afternoon before to run the dozens of small errands necessary before she could pack for her trip, and she had neglected to put gas in it. Walking ten blocks to the nearest gas station with the chill wind of December penetrating her lightweight suit jacket, whipping her hair, and blowing fine Texas sand from the streets into her face did not improve Anne's temper.

Metcalf Caterers was not the largest catering firm in Dallas, but it was growing, and in the five years it had been in existence had built up a select clientele. Anne had been with the husband-and-wife team, Joe and Iva, for three of those years. Starting as secretary-receptionist, she had gradually become much more than that. She turned her hand to anything from marketing to serving at tables. She could blend a sauce, decorate a cake, arrange a centerpiece, or balance the books with equal ease, and as Iva Metcalf told her with a wry grin, look as if she were enjoying it. Usually she did just that, but there were days ...

"Where have you been?" Iva exclaimed in pained accents as Anne came through the glass doors of the reception room at last.

"You will never believe what I have been through this morning ..." Anne began.

Iva shook her close-cropped red head. "Don't bet on it. This telephone hasn't stopped ringing since I got here. Mrs. Burson, the woman who has the luncheon today, called to inform us that of the twelve guests she will be entertaining, one is allergic to tomatoes, one to eggs, and one can't abide the sight of mushrooms. She just thought we might like to know. Mrs. Otley, whose daughter is to marry the oil millionaire this evening, wants an oil derrick as an arch over the bride and groom on top of the cake she ordered, and Señor Ramón Carlos Castillo's secretary called to inform us that the señor has canceled his dinner party planned for tonight at his hotel suite. He is flying back to Mexico City late this evening because of illness in the family—it's his grandmother—and he would like a simple dinner delivered to his private jet at the airport before seven o'clock. He doesn't want anything elaborate since he will be traveling alone, without his usual steward, private secretary, and half-dozen flunkeys, just something he can heat and serve himself; a trout marguery, fresh asparagus, fresh pears—out of season, of course—and a bottle of chilled white wine."

"Good grief," Anne said faintly.

"Exactly so."

Turning to hang up her shoulder bag and coat in the closet, Anne asked, "Don't these people ever eat anything simple, like a ham sandwich?"

"If they did, we would be out of business," Iva replied. "Anyway, men like Señor Castillo can afford the best. Why shouldn't they have it?"

"It seems such a waste, all that time and trouble for one man when he could have solved the whole thing by buying himself a loaf of bread and a package of sandwich meat."

"You mean have his chauffeur stop for it on the way to the airport? Your trouble, Anne dear, is you don't think big enough."

"No doubt you're right," Anne agreed with a wry grimace. "What do we tackle first?"

"If you will see to Mrs. Otley's oil derrick, I'll start the search for the señor's trout and pears. We must pamper our largest account. Keep your head down as you go into the kitchen, though. Tony is not in the best of humors after having to rearrange his menus, and he's threatening to quit again, of course. If you can manage to work your usual magic at calming him down, I will be eternally grateful."

Tony was their chef, and as such, a man to be placated at all costs. A french Creole from Louisiana, he had learned his art in some of the great kitchens of France. Returning to his native New Orleans with the title of cordon-bleu, he had worked for ten years in one of the most famous restaurants in that city. He had left to start a small restaurant of his own, but the venture had not been a success. One reason was his insistence on quality; only the best was good enough to go into his culinary creations, and not enough people were willing to pay the cost. Another reason was his temper. He was apt to take anything the diners left on their plates as a personal affront to his skill, and it was not unknown for him to charge out of the kitchen and demand what was wrong with a particular dish. To have anyone question or change his menus also raised his ire, and Anne was not surprised, when she passed through the doors that led to the chrome and white-enamel kitchens of the catering service, to find him chopping shallots with vicious precision and casting them into a skillet with all the muttered maledictions of a sorcerer brewing poison. Buttoning herself into the orange nylon cover-up she wore while in the kitchen, she summoned a smile and set herself to the task of soothing Tony.

She found time in the middle of the morning for a cup of coffee and a sweet roll, but she had to eat standing up. Finally the luncheon menu of baked red snapper in a brown oyster sauce, broccoli au gratin, Metcalf's special home-baked french loaves, and French chocolate silk pie was complete. It was Iva and her husband, Joe's job to transport it to the home of Mrs. Burson, where her kitchen staff would serve it. But eleven o'clock came and went with no Iva. Then, just as Anne was sliding into the front seat of the van, Iva's station wagon came wheeling into the parking lot. She stepped out on the run, threw a package wrapped with butcher paper and a couple of brown paper bags into Anne's arms. "Paint it with black spray paint," she called, scrambling into the van, and then she was gone.

The butcher wrap contained three nice trout. In the bags were three fresh ripe pears with just a blush of pink on their tender green skins, and a white plastic replica of an oil derrick.

Sprayed black, the derrick looked hideous towering over the poor little bride and groom dolls on top of a cake four layers tall. Painting it silver instead was slightly better, but Anne still thought, as she helped settle it into the van late that afternoon, that the best thing to be done with it was tear it off and toss it in the trash can. Cases of champagne, cans of nuts and mints, the ingredients for the firm's secret recipe bridal punch, and an assortment of hors d'oeuvres packed in white cardboard boxes had already been loaded. It was with a distinct feeling of relief that Anne watched Joe and Iva pull out of the parking lot with that assignment. Now all that was left was the señor's supper, and this terrible day would be over. The weekend would be hers, two whole days to loaf, read, wash her hair, and recover from this ordeal.

The trout marguery sat cooling, filling the air with an aroma so delectable it was all Anne could do not to sit down and devour it; the asparagus, exquisitely tender, had been anointed with butter; the French loaves were wrapped in their heavy linen napkin; the pears nestled in a nest of tissue in a small woven basket; and the wine, a dry chablis, sat cooling in its disposable plastic cooler. Tony, his duty done, threw down his chef's hat and went home, and his two helpers, after clearing the kitchen and putting the dishes away, were not long in following him.

By a quarter after six Anne was growing anxious. The meal was due on board the plane at seven o'clock sharp. It would not do to disappoint their best customer. Anne had never met him personally, but from comments Iva had made from time to time, she thought Señor Castillo would not be the kind of man to easily forgive those who had failed him.

The jangle of the telephone cut across her thoughts. With a quiver of apprehension along her nerves, she reached for it. At the sound of Iva's voice, she let out the breath she had caught in a sigh of purest relief. It was short-lived.

"Anne, I hate to tell you, but Joe and I are hung up over here. There's been a five-car pileup on the Interstate and the traffic is so snarled up we won't be able to move for hours."

"Where are you calling from?" Anne asked, aware of the noise of a car's engine in the background.

"There was a nice man three or four cars ahead of us with a phone in his car and he patched the call through for me. I don't know what I would have done without him; it must be miles to the nearest public phone. But never mind about that. It looks like you are going to have to run Señor Castillo's dinner out to the airport. You do have your roommate's car, don't you? Good. I'm going to call ahead and clear the way with the airport officials for you. According to what the secretary said on the phone this morning, there is only one thing to remember, and that's to be sure everything is put away when you leave; that is, don't leave anything lying about loose that might slide around or fall during takeoff."

"Yes, but where—"

"I have no idea," Iva replied cheerfully before Anne could complete her question. "Joe and I have always put the food in the hands of the señor's steward, but apparently the man was given the weekend off and couldn't get back to Dallas in time for this unscheduled flight. Don't worry about it. You'll find where everything goes. It can't be too difficult; an airplane galley is just a small kitchen and you ought to know your way around one of those if anybody does!"

"It can't be too difficult—" That was Iva's opinion, Anne thought with something like bitterness. In the first place, Anne had never been on a plane in her life, much less a private jet, and the sight of that great silver monster sitting on the runway in the dusk with its lights blinking and its jets screaming was enough to bring her heart into her throat. She had never walked up to an entrance ramp barred by an armed guard either. She wished that she had thought to keep on her orange jacket with Metcalf's printed on the pocket. She had left it behind in the kitchen by force of habit, since she did not intend to return there before going on home.

She was half-afraid the guard would demand some form of identification, which could be a problem. She had locked her shoulder bag, a large, cumbersome affair of fringe and burlap, in the car, to leave her hands free.

The only thing of value in it was her driver's license and a gas credit card. Because Joe and Iva had not returned, she had not been paid for this week.

Her fears did not materialize. Seeing the laden tray in her hands, the guard gave her a nod and a smile as if she were not unexpected. Touching his cap, he stepped aside, motioning her aboard without attempting to speak over the noise of the jets.

Just inside the plane was a small section fitted with seats much like a commercial jet, but since Iva had said the galley was in the rear, Anne moved along the aisle between the seats past a shelf arranged with the latest magazines and a small alcove where wraps could be put away. Pushing with her tray through a pair of heavy drapes in maroon and black brocade, she stepped into the main body of the plane. For an instant, she stood still, surveying the large cabin that stretched before her. Short drapes of brocade were looped back from the small windows. A carpet of thick, lustrous maroon velvet covered the floor. At intervals down one side of its expanse sat round walnut tables flanked by deep, comfortable chairs of black leather. On the other side was a long walnut desk fitted with a built-in phone and dictating machine, and with a walnut and leather chair behind it. The remaining space was taken up by an extra-wide settee which at that moment was made up as a bed with a pillow and sheets in heavy ivory linen, monogrammed in black.

Lifting an eyebrow in token of her amazement, Anne continued through the cabin to a small metal door half-concealed by more drapes at the far end of the plane.

The noise of the jets warming up for flight was nerve-shattering in this section, especially when the cabin door swung to behind her. Anne would have liked very much to plunk the tray down and leave, but remembering her instructions, she began to look for a place to secure the contents. The wine fitted very nicely into the refrigerator unit with its cooler intact. There was a food warmer with a snap-down lid that held the hot entrée and vegetable, and after a few minutes of searching, she found a bread box that pulled out of the wall. Giving herself a mental pat on the back, she was just turning to go when she noticed several cardboard cases stacked on the floor. Close examination showed them to be small glass bottles of grape juice. What a Mexican millionaire could possibly want with four cases of grape juice posed something of a mystery, but it had obviously been delivered by someone who assumed the steward would be there to put it away. There would be quite a mess to clean up if those bottles were to break in flight. It couldn't take more than a moment to put them out of harm's way.

Or could it? Every cabinet she opened seemed to be filled already with china and crystal in neat restraining racks, and with foodstuff in cans and boxes and plastic bags. Those drawers and cabinets that were not being used for normal purposes were filled with papers, bound account books, and boxes of letterhead, pens, and recording tapes. She was just about to give up and let the señor attend to his own grape juice when she found an empty shelf. It was above her head however, and it would take a great deal of effort to lift the cases up onto it, especially with the restraining ledge in place. It would be much easier, she thought, if she had something to stand on. In a cubbyhole between the refrigerator and the bank of cabinets that served as a pantry was a postage stamp of a table with a lightweight straight-backed chair on each side. The chairs, she found, were fastened to the floor, but a moment's study enabled her to decipher the simple locking mechanism. As she swung the chair where she needed it, she found herself hoping rather grimly that Señor Castillo appreciated the extra trouble that Metcalf's was willing to go to for his sake. Then she laughed at herself as she realized that the señor would probably never learn of it.

She was just settling the last case of juice when something in the shrieking roar of the jets caught at her attention. The sound had changed, gradually increasing. A vibration ran through the plane, setting the dishes in the cabinets around her to clinking with a soft regularity. And then as she stood in frozen stillness, she felt it. They were moving!

Panic galvanized her muscles. She dropped the juice case into place, slammed the cabinet door, and turned away. If she called out, it was doubtful anyone would hear her. She had to make her way as quickly as possible to the pilot's cabin. No, wait. If they were taking off, the señor must have boarded the plane. He would be in the main cabin just beyond the door.

Consternation flooded over her as she touched one hand to the cabinet front and started to step down from the chair. In that instant a surge of power gripped the plane and the floor tilted, slanting upward. The movement threw Anne off balance. She clutched wildly at a cabinet door handle as she felt herself falling, but her fingers would not hold. The top of the small table flashed across her vision, and the corner of it caught her squarely on the temple. Blinding pain struck deep into her brain and a soft darkness came up from the floor to catch her.

It might have been only a moment or two, it might have been half an hour, before Anne opened her eyes. For a dazed instant she could not understand why she was lying wedged between a table and refrigerator or why her head was throbbing with a furious pain allied to a steady humming noise. Remembering was not pleasant.

Slowly she levered herself into a sitting position.

Nothing seemed to be broken, but there was a huge lump on the side of her head that ached to the touch. The plane had leveled off, and she could get to her feet without too much difficulty. The movement sent a wave of dizziness over her, however, and she subsided quickly into the remaining chair on the opposite side of the table. She would sit there for just a moment, and then she must find some way of letting someone know of her presence.

The opening of the small metal door between the galley and the main cabin did not immediately penetrate her consciousness. Awareness came with a sense of tingling disquiet. Combating a strange reluctance, she raised her head, and stared into the black eyes, lit by tawny flames of rage, of the man standing in the doorway. Her heart increased its beat, giving her a smothering sensation. For long moments she could not move, could not withdraw her gaze. And then, raking her pale face with his dark, feline glance, he drawled, "Airsick already? Too bad, but a fitting punishment for a stowaway."

Shock rippled through her. Unconsciously she straightened, drawing a deep, reviving breath. "I'm not a stowaway."

"Don't trouble to deny it. This plane is definitely not public transportation; it belongs to me. There is not one of my employees who would dare to smuggle you aboard without my permission, and as I did not extend you an invitation . . ." he paused suggestively.

The sarcasm overlying the softly dangerous timbre of his voice made little impression on Anne. Her eyes widened a fraction. So this was Señor Ramón Carlos Castillo. She pictured the Mexican millionaire in her mind, for some reason, as short, plump, and graying. Nothing could have been further from the truth. His lithe frame filled the doorway, marking him as above-average height. No trace of gray threaded the blue-blackness of his hair, though from the fine lines that radiated from the corners of his eyes she thought he must be at least a few years over thirty. He had removed the coat of his suit, loosening his tie and opening the collar of his shirt. In contrast to the fine white silk, his skin had the golden swarthiness of an ancient Aztec idol. The planes of his face were rigid with the same impassive contempt she had seen once in a carving of their sun god.

"No more protests?" he queried, one corner of his firm mouth lifting in a mirthless smile as he moved into the galley. "Then perhaps you would like to tell me why you have foisted yourself on me?"

His presence in that tiny compartment was overpowering. Though he came to a stop with the heel of his hand resting on the refrigerator, he seemed to loom over her. She could not meet his fierce eyes, fastening her gaze instead on the signet ring on his little finger, a ring in black enamel on gold featuring the head of a small tiger. She wished she did not feel so disoriented. She could hardly expect him to be as concerned as she was over her predicament; still, his obvious anger and suspicion confused her.

With a supreme effort, she gathered her thoughts. In a voice that sounded weak even to her own ears she said, "I am sorry for the inconvenience to you, but could you please tell your pilot to turn the plane around and go back?"

"A time-consuming operation. Tell me why I should do that?"

She stared at him for a blank moment before answering, "Because . . . I have to get off."

"Why? Hasn't your welcome been what you expected?" he asked, a soft tone in his voice that she did not like. His accent was very slight, she realized, more an intonation than anything else. Under other circumstances it might have been attractive.

"I—didn't expect a welcome of any kind," she faltered.

"Are you certain? Are you quite certain you did not expect . . . this?" He leaned toward her with a swift, sure movement, encircling her waist, dragging her to her feet and against his chest. The grim mask of his face hovered above her, an odd, questing light in his black eyes, and then his mouth came down on hers.

Anne had never had much time for romance. She had had a brief flirtation or two, shared a few good-night kisses, but nothing more serious. She had never been kissed like this, never felt the burning force of barely leashed passion, never been held in a crushing embrace from which she could not have escaped, even if she had desired it. More in surprise than response, her lips parted beneath his, and then in the recesses of her mind she recognized the emotion that drove him. It was contempt.

His hold had slackened as he felt her complaisance. Abruptly Anne drew back, tearing herself out of his arms.

Señor Castillo retained his grip on her wrist. "Wasn't your welcome to your liking?" he asked, sarcasm edging his voice.

Anger erupted inside Anne's brain, crowding out shock and confusion, subduing for a brief instant the pain that still pulsed there. Her eyes blazing in her pale face, she lifted her free hand and struck out at the hateful, mocking face above her. She never reached her target. Her arm was caught, turned, and once more she found herself held against the silk-clad chest of the señor. Resistance, she discovered, was futile.

Panting with her struggles, she flung back her head, shaking the tawny gold hair out of her face. "Let me go," she said through gritted teeth.

He surveyed her, an expression in his eyes that made her far too aware of the quick rise and fall of her breasts against him. A muscle in the hard line of his jaw tightened, then suddenly she was free. She stepped back a quick pace, rubbing her wrists where his fingers had bitten into the flesh. A continuous tremor ran through her, and she clenched her hands to keep their trembling from becoming obvious to this man who stared down at her. It was rage, she told herself only rage.

"Well," he gibed.

She looked up at him in mute incomprehension.

"Aren't you going to favor me with the excuse you made up for the occasion? Or didn't you even intend to try to explain why you are here?"

Anne took a deep breath. "I am here," she told him as calmly as she could manage, "because your secretary placed an order with Metcalf Caterers. We were to deliver a light dinner to your plane. I brought it."

"You will forgive me if I point out that you don't have the look of a caterer?" he said dryly.

"Looks have nothing to do with it—" she began, only to be interrupted.

"Still, I suppose you are fully prepared to tell me what Metcalf's has sent for my delectation?"

She was, of course. She had been just about to present her knowledge of the menu as proof positive of her story. The implication that such a move was expected, and would, therefore, carry little weight, brought a flush to her cheeks. But what could she do? There was nothing else she could use to convince him. She told him, in considerable detail, the contents of the refrigerator and the warmer.

"Very good." He applauded. "You have used your time while hidden back here to excellent advantage. I congratulate you on your intelligence. It seems to be superior to the average of the women who usually try such bizarre methods to bring themselves to my attention."

Anne clung to her temper with difficulty. "I did not come aboard this plane to bring myself to your attention," she said evenly. "In fact, I can't think of anything I would be less likely to do. Why any woman would want to put herself in such a humiliating position is more than I can understand."

"I don't understand it either, but there it is. Rock stars, movie stars, men of power, position, and wealth affect young women in strange ways. I have had women accost me in hotel rooms, on the beach, the golf course, and tennis court. They wait in my limousine if it is left unguarded for an instant. On one memorable occasion I was invaded in a sauna bath. So you see, you are not the only one who has tried this ruse, though I will grant that you are the first to stowaway on my plane. You must tell me how you managed it."

"I did not stowaway," Anne said, her voice rising, "and furthermore, I doubt that half the other women you claim have been throwing themselves at you had any such intention. You are the most arrogant, conceited, obstinate man I have ever come across—"

"I never claimed the attraction was anything more than my money," he interposed with a slight smile. But ignoring his comment, she rushed on.

"And I would have been perfectly happy if I had never set eyes on you! And I wouldn't have if it hadn't been for those ridiculous cases of grape juice I found stacked up on the floor. If I hadn't stopped to put them away, I would have been gone long before you came on board! Though what use," she ended bitterly, "a man who ordered wine with his dinner can have for so many bottles of grape juice is more than I can see."

"For my grandmother," he murmured, an arrested look in his dark eyes. "She has a preference for that brand only."

Anne's face cleared as that small mystery was solved.

"I see, for the one who is ill," she said before she thought.

His features hardened immediately. "That is correct. You really must tell me your sources of information. In the meantime I suggest you come into the cabin and make yourself comfortable for the remainder of the flight."

"You are going to turn back?" Anne asked, driven by a distinct feeling of misgiving.

The señor had already turned toward the cabin door. Now he swung back. "Unfortunately not."

"You can't mean—you don't mean that you are going on to Mexico City."

"I mean exactly that. We are already nearly an hour into a flight that normally takes approximately two and a quarter hours. To turn back would be a waste of time, fuel, and money, but especially time, which may be of the essence."

"But I can't go to Mexico City with you! I have no money with me, no papers. How will I get back to Dallas? And if I can't get back, how can I stay? I haven't a change of clothing, not even a toothbrush."

"You should have thought of that before you smuggled yourself on board."

"I did not smuggle myself on this plane," she grated. "I walked on with the tray from Metcalf's. If you don't believe me, you can ask the guard who was stationed at the foot of the gangway."

"That is your first mistake, señorita. You know very well there was no guard—that he was called away to assist with a heart-attack victim on one of the commercial airliners. Which is the only reason you are here."

She might have guessed there was some such reason why the guard had not informed the señor that she was still on board. What was the use of arguing? What difference did it make what Señor Castillo believed? With luck she would never see him again. When she reached Mexico City, perhaps she could throw herself on the mercy of the airport officials, and if she explained what had happened, maybe they would put her on a return flight to Dallas. Failing that, there was always the American consulate. They would surely help her to get in touch with Joe and Iva. These tentative plans forming in her mind, she marched before him into the cabin and seated herself in one of the cushioned lounge chairs.

It was a little unnerving to have the señor, instead of returning to the rumpled comfort of the settee made up as a bed for him, lower his long length into the chair across from her. She tried to ignore his close scrutiny by staring out the nearest window at the twilight purple of the late-evening sky with the cloud layer just below them shot with the gold of the last rays of the sun reaching from beyond the edge of the horizon. It was a beautiful sight and one that was oddly soothing. When, after a time, Señor Castillo spoke, she was able to turn to him with at least an appearance of composure.

"You have someone who will be worried when you do not return this evening?" he queried. "Your parents, perhaps?"

Her roommate, Judy, was out of town. Joe and Iva would not expect to see her again until Monday morning. No, there was no one. She shook her head.

The face of the man across from her turned a shade harder and the brooding silence fell once more.

"What is your name?" he asked abruptly.

She struggled for a brief moment with the impulse to tell him it was none of his business. She could foresee no good in making him the gift of it. She wanted no more to do with Señor Castillo than she could help. In truth, the quicker she forgot the entire day leading up to this moment, the happier she would be. There might, however, be one thing to be gained by withholding it.

"Why?" she inquired.

The inclination of his head was a masterpiece of irony. "You have a slight advantage of me," he replied.

The recessed lighting of the cabin was dim. It gave a soft sheen to her tawny hair and made mysterious pools of her gold-flecked eyes as she faced him. "If you want to know my name," she said slowly, "you can ask at Metcalf Caterers."

He stared at her, his eyes narrowed speculatively under thick dark brows; then he gave a quick, impatient shake of his head. With an abrupt change of subject he asked, "Have you had dinner?"

She was forced to admit she had not.

"Nor have I," he rejoined shortly. "Since you have inspected the provisions made by Metcalf's, you should have some idea if there is enough food for two?"

"Yes, I think so," she answered, adding quickly, "It is Metcalf's policy to give ample portions."

"Spare me the corroborating statements," he requested with a sharp gesture as he got to his feet. "I am asking you to share a meal with me, no more than that."

Anne would have liked to have refused to eat with him, but that would have been foolhardy. She had eaten only the sketchiest kind of lunch, a half of a sandwich and a cup of coffee, more than eight hours ago, and there was no way of knowing when she would be able to eat again since she had no money with her. Moreover, the smell of the trout marguery, when her host removed the cover from the container, would have shaken a much stronger will than her own. While she searched for china, silver, and a glass for the señor's wine, he meticulously divided the fare into two equal portions. He insisted that she have wine also, finding the glass and filling it for her when she demurred. She was not accustomed to wine with her meals, and the first taste of the sparkling, pale-gold liquid sat oddly on her palate, but as she gradually grew used to it, it seemed right for the time and the place. It was not easy to force the first few bites of food down her throat that was tight with nerves. She was helped considerably, in time, by the señor's attitude. Concentrating on his dinner and, afterward, staring into his wineglass, he gave every appearance of having forgotten she was there.

It was, she discovered, a false impression. No sooner had she drained her wineglass than he leaned to refill it.

"No, please. Really, I don't want it," she protested. He paid no attention, tipping the last of the bottle into her glass. The idea flitted across her mind that he was trying to make her tipsy, then she had to suppress a smile at the absurdity of it. Nothing was less likely.

"Drink it," he told her, his gaze on her long, slender fingers playing in a nervous gesture with the stem of the wineglass. "It will help you relax."

"I don't need to relax," she said, flicking him a puzzled glance from under her lashes.

"Don't you? I would have thought there was something troubling you. Are you certain there is no one at home who will care what becomes of you?"

The wording of his phrase disturbed her. Immediately on the defensive, she answered, "Only for tonight. I have a roommate who will be back tomorrow. Naturally she will be concerned if I'm not at the apartment." It would be late Sunday evening before Judy returned, but Señor Ramón Carlos Castillo did not need to know that.

"She? This roommate is a young woman?"

"Of course," Anne replied, a shade of tartness creeping into her voice.

The señor raised a brow. "Your pardon," he drawled.

"These days such a thing cannot be taken for granted. What of your parents, then? Are they so modern they take no notice where you go or when you return?"

"I fail to see what concern it is of yours," Anne said, lifting her chin, "but my parents are dead. In any case, I am over twenty-one and have been taking care of myself for some time."

The señor nodded. "I begin to see."

As she caught the trend of his reasoning, a frustrated anger such as she had never felt before rose up in Anne. He thought that, because she had been orphaned, she was a girl with some kind of obsessive need for the kind of security he represented. In her rage and chagrin she could not decide which was worse, to be thought mercenary or merely pathetic.

Glaring at him, she said distinctly, "You do not see anything, anything at all!"

When he smiled into her stormy brown eyes, she could have reached out and slapped his golden, sardonic face—if she had not been afraid.

Chapter 2

In a silence that was something less than friendly, they cleared away the remains of the meal and placed the dishes and utensils in the cushioned plastic holders that would keep them unbroken until they could be washed after landing. This done, the señor escorted her back into the main cabin, then took his leave, saying he wished to speak to his pilot.

Anne was glad enough to be relieved of his presence. She sank back into one of the armchairs, resting her head on the soft, pillowed back, wondering dejectedly what she was going to do. It was a frightening situation. Suppose Señor Castillo decided to press charges? What chance would she have to explain her position in a foreign language? And even if there was someone available who could understand her, what chance did she have that Mexican officialdom would believe her against one of their own countrymen? Even if the worst did not occur, what would she do after being set down in a strange country? How could she contact Joe and Iva without money to pay for a wire or phone call? If she was forced to turn to the American consulate, there was always the possibility they would not come to her assistance. She had heard they were no longer so helpful to stranded Americans, especially young people, as they had once been. Too many teenagers touring foreign countries by means of their thumbs had turned to the embassies to bail them out when they ran into difficulties. It did no good to worry about it. She would just have to wait and see.

With a conscious effort, she directed her thoughts into other channels. Was the señor married, she wondered. She had never heard Iva mention a wife. In fact, she thought she remembered her saying that the wife of one of his American business partners usually acted as his hostess when he was in Dallas. That could mean nothing, of course. Perhaps Señora Castillo did not like to travel? Perhaps there were children at home in school she could not leave, or small ones who could not have their routines upset by the difficulties of traveling back and forth? If so, it meant frequent separation, something she, if she were in his wife's place, would not like. Not that he would allow his wife's likes and dislikes to weigh very heavily with him, the poor woman.

It was ridiculous. What did she care about his domestic arrangements? The wine she had drunk must have gone to her head. She would be much better off if she could use this opportunity to get a little rest. It had been a hectic day. Perhaps if she could relax a little her headache would go away. An aspirin would help, but she could not bring herself to ask the señor for one. It had too much the sound of trying to gain his sympathy. She closed her eyes.

She awakened to find Señor Castillo bending over her, his face inches from her own. Her eyes widening, she pressed back against the seat, then flushed as an amused derision curled the corner of his mouth. Calmly, he continued fastening her seat belt. "Such a shame to disturb you," he said, his gaze on his hands as he tested the tightness of the belt across her lap, "but we are coming into Mexico City—or simply Mexico, as the residents of our capital call her."

Nodding both her thanks and her comprehension, Anne turned to the window. Below were the far-flung lights of a great city lying in a valley encircled by the dark ring of a mountain range. The lights danced and shimmered through a haze of clouds, and feeling the sharp downward slant of the plane, she knew a moment's apprehension. A glance at the señor, buckling himself into the opposite seat without concern, was enough to allay her fears. He leaned back and, as the cabin light slanted across his features, Anne thought he looked tired and dispirited.

"Is—is your grandmother very bad?" she asked after a moment.

"I have no way of knowing. I assume so, or I would not have been summoned."

The faint note of impatience in his voice was enough to discourage further questions. Anne murmured, "I'm sorry," and fell silent.

The landing was smooth and uneventful. The night air that greeted them as they disembarked was cool and fresh, and, above the smell of dust and fuel oil, perfumed with a scent reminiscent of attar of roses. They were met by a slight young man carrying a pad and pen who might have been a secretary, and also a uniformed official. Neither were introduced. With the señor's hand under her elbow, Anne walked with the three men into the airport terminal. There she was shown into a small, comfortably furnished lounge, and before she could either ask for an explanation or make her own, she was left alone.

An hour passed with excruciating slowness, and then another. She leafed through the magazines that were available, but since they were printed in Spanish, they could not occupy her for long. Plaques on the wall representing a smiling sun and the frowning moon caught her interest and she studied them minutely. They appeared handmade with excellent craftsmanship, as did an ashtray on a carved teakwood table that she took to be a reproduction in turquoise-colored mica of the Aztec calendar stone. She smiled a little, touching her fingertips to the roughness of the ashtray. It might be as close as she would ever come to the real thing.

She had just convinced herself, for the third time, that she had better take matters into her own hands and begin making her own arrangements, when the señor returned.

"My apologies for keeping you waiting," he said, holding the door for her. "Everything is in order. We can go."

Anne did not move. "Go where?" she asked bluntly.

"To my home. There is no commercial flight to Dallas until well into the morning. I offer you the hospitality of my house until that time."

The stiff formality of his last phrase was not unbecoming to him. Neither did it imply a very warm welcome. "I think I would prefer to stay here at the airport until the flight is called," she said.

"It would be most uncomfortable. Besides, you will miss your breakfast," he reminded her.

Lifting her chin, she replied. "I'm sure that won't hurt me."

"Maybe not, but it offends my sense of hospitality," he returned, a small smile curving his mouth.

"I would prefer not to be obligated to you any more than necessary. You must know I cannot pay you for my return ticket just now, but if you will give me your address, I will send the money to you as soon as I can." It had been a difficult speech. It was irritating to see how little effect it had on him.

"Surely there can be no need. If you are the innocent victim you claim, a return ticket and a night's hospitality are the least I owe you by way of reparation for carrying you off against your will, and if you are not, then shouldn't you be ready and eager to take advantage of what I may offer you?"

Anne eyed him warily. "I thought you had little use for the women who 'foisted themselves on you.'"

His brows lifted a fraction and a silver gleam shone in the depths of his eyes as he replied, "I don't remember saying that."

"But your attitude . . ." she protested.

". . . depends on the woman," he ended. "But why worry? Such matters have nothing to do with you, do they?"

"No," she answered in as firm a voice as she could manage.

"Well, then? What need have you to distrust my hospitality?" His tone hardened. "It may help you to know that my grandmother is in residence with me. I assure you my thoughts at the moment are for her alone. I feel also that I have delayed long enough here at this time. The car is waiting. May we please go?"

At the reminder of his grandmother's illness, color swept into Anne's face. "Yes, I'm sorry," she said in distress, moving toward him.

"There is no need for such remorse," he told her, the sternness of his features relenting as he smiled. "I have put a call through to my home in San Angel on the outskirts of the city and they tell me she is sleeping comfortably."

Anne slanted a thoughtful glance at him as she walked beside him to the long, sleek car—and its driver, the bespectacled secretary—that waited for them outside the terminal. For reasons of his own, he had made it almost impossible to refuse to accompany him to his home for the night without seeming both ridiculous and ungrateful. Why had he gone to the trouble? Was it only an example of the famous Spanish hospitality, or was his reason entirely different? Was she a fool for agreeing so easily to go with him? No, surely not. A man like Señor Castillo had no need to force his attentions on a woman. Only an idiot would suppose that he might. And yet, she could not forget the kiss he had taken so effortlessly, or the helplessness she had felt in his arms. She felt a shiver over the surface of her skin, a primitive instinct of danger, one she could ignore at her own risk.

Mexico City, even at this late hour, was far from being asleep. Cars flowed in a steady stream along the side streets, moving at incredible speeds, with taxicabs in various stages of dilapidation darting in and out, and men and boys on bicycles pedaling doggedly along in desperate danger to life and limb. At some of the intersections on the street called the Paseo de la Reforma were traffic circles like enormous revolving doors in which it seemed they might be caught forever. People strolled along the streets, the men for the most part in business suits and the women conventionally dressed, though here and there could be seen the traditional sombrero and serape against the cool night air of the mountains and an older woman with her head wrapped in a somber-colored rebozo. There were the ornate, carved fronts of old colonial-era buildings, towering skyscrapers glittering with glass and bright lights, the impressive, well-guarded portals of luxury hotels, and the bases of stone monuments whose figures were lost in the darkness above them. And then the hustle of main streets was behind them and they entered narrow, winding streets marked with small blue and white signs on the sides of buildings indicating one-way traffic. This was an older residential section with trees lining the streets and leaning over the high, whitewashed, vine-covered walls of secluded, private homes.

Once, as they slowed to turn, Anne caught a glimpse of a church, its old, tiled domes shining blue and yellow in the glow of a fitful moon. Seeing the direction of her gaze, the señor told her, "The convent church of Nuestra Señora del Carmen."

Realizing that she had been craning to see everything like the most impressionable tourist, Anne sat back. "I love old buildings," she said by way of explanation, but as he smiled without replying, she found her own mouth curving into an unabashed grin. It was tremendously exciting to be in a foreign city, a city she had never dreamed she would be able to visit. She sincerely hoped that there in the dimness of the car she did not have too much the look of the cat with canary feathers on its chin.

The car slowed, swung wide for a turn, and came to a halt before a pair of wide, wrought-iron gates set into a stretch of whitewashed wall. The driver blew a short summons on the horn. Almost immediately an elderly man shuffled into view and, unlocking the chain that held them, threw the gates open.

A cobblestone drive was revealed curving around the main house toward a small building that had the look of a carriage house converted to use as a garage. In the beam of the headlights the drive appeared to cut through the meticulously kept expanse of a garden. Shrubs, vines, and climbing roses swept up to the walls of the dwelling, crowding about the arched colonnade on the lower of its two floors and casting lacy shadows on its ancient plastered walls. It was a massive building formed in the shape of a hollow square around a central patio, with wrought-iron grills over the lower outside windows and closed jalousies like sleeping eyes along the top floor. An enormous oil lantern illuminated the deep carving of the heavy wooden entrance door.

At a sign from Señor Castillo, the car drew to a stop before the stone walkway that led to the front door. Alighting, the señor helped Anne out. The car slid away just as the front door was thrown open, spilling a square of light toward them like a welcome mat.

"Ah, María," the señor exclaimed, catching sight of

the short, squat woman framed in the opening. A brief conversation in rapid Spanish followed as they stepped inside, then the señor turned to introduce Anne to the woman.

"Miss Matthews, this is my housekeeper, María. She will show you to your room and make you comfortable. If there is anything you need, you have only to ask for it."

Murmuring her thanks, Anne smiled at the Spanish woman in her black dress covered by a white apron trimmed with red embroidery. No answering smile warmed that austere, censorious face. The woman turned in the direction of a wide staircase with polished treads and heavily carved balusters that rose against one wall of the entrance hall. Anne, preparing to follow her, glanced curiously at the wainscoted walls topped by wide expanses of cool white plaster enlivened by paintings.

The ceiling was high, ornamented with a wide, molded frieze and a center medallion. Hanging from this by a thick chain was a chandelier of dark wood and multicolored glass. The colors were repeated in the glowing amber, red, brown, and black of the Persian carpet lying beneath it on the floor. There was a scent in the air of roses, the beeswax used to polish furniture, and the indefinable smell of old buildings.

"María?" the señor called. When the woman halted and turned, he continued in Spanish that carried the firm tone of command.

"Sí, señor," the woman replied when he finished speaking, though her face, if possible, seemed set in lines of even deeper disapproval.

Anne looked from the señor to his housekeeper. Mistrust gathered in her gold-flecked eyes. "What did you tell her?" she asked.

"I only directed her to put you in the French bedroom," he said, his expression perfectly serious except for the mocking lift of one dark brow. "It is a room in the portion of the house farthest from that of my grandmother so that the noise of your arrival and departure will not disturb her. What María finds not to her liking is that it is also only one door removed from my own bedroom. You must forgive her. She is not used to her master bringing young, attractive women of unexplained background home with him. Also, she is from the country, from the *quinta*, or farm, of my ancestors, and easily shocked."

"I must see what I can do to put her mind at rest then," Anne told him.

"Try, by all means," he answered with a slight inclination of his head, "though you may find it hard going. María has no English."

Annoyance brought a flush of color to Anne's cheeks. "You could make the situation plain to her if you wanted to."

"So I could, if I were willing to discuss my affairs with my servants, or allow them to be the arbiters of my actions."

There was no answer to that. Compressing her lips, Anne turned away, but the arrogance stamped on his dark Spanish-Indian features remained in her memory for some time.

The bedroom she was shown into was not what she had expected. Considering the Spanish colonial style of the rest of the house, she had thought to find something similar, though perhaps not so darkly ornamental. Instead, she discovered elegance. The bed was a creation of brass and bone china with four posts, the two at the head rising to form a half-canopy. The china fittings on the posts, the footboard, and headboard were painted with delicate nosegays of pink roses and violets. Rose silk bedhangings were draped from the half-canopy, and drapes of the same material hung at the windows over muslin undercurtains. The

dressing table and wardrobe had the graceful lines of
the Louis-Quinze period, a style that blended perfectly
with the cream and green and rose of the Aubusson
rug.

The amenities in the connecting bath were in keeping with the decor. The washbasin of white china had
a rim of tiny pink roses above a swirl of painted gold
ribbon. The tub stood on legs of an antique design,
and the handles of the fixtures were in the shape of
scrolls.

An expression on her face of the same stolid endurance as a man going before the firing squad, María indicated fluffy pink towels and washcloths, bath salts,
soap, and a drawer containing toothbrushes still in
their wrappers, and small tubes of paste. A hairbrush of
pristine cleanliness was brought out, then the woman
went to the wardrobe to remove a nightgown of palest
flesh-pink silk. A faint perfume of potpourri was wafted
into the air as María laid it across the bed. Under the
spell of such an old-fashioned scent, it was a moment
before Anne realized that though the skirt of the gown
was long and flowing, the bodice was composed of
nothing more than a cobweb of lace. It didn't matter, of
course. There would be no one to see her in it. Still,
that vague sense of mistrust she had felt earlier assailed
her once more.

"Buenas noches, señorita," María said from the
doorway.

Collecting herself with an effort, Anne told the
woman goodnight and, when she had gone, carefully
locked the door behind her.

A warm, lingering bath made a great improvement
to her jangled nerves. By the time she had padded
around in her bare feet, folding her cream drill skirt
and jacket, and her orange shell over a chair, rinsing
out her underclothing and hanging them to drip-dry,
some of the strangeness of her surroundings had worn

away. She could never really get used to such luxury, she mused as she caught sight of herself in the oval mirror with its candle sidelights over the dressing table. She was not meant for such things. She had to admit, however, that nothing she had ever owned had become her like the graceful wisp of the gown she was wearing. The color seemed to lend a pearllike sheen to her skin and to bring a richer gleam to the gold highlights in her tawny blond hair. A faint color bloomed in the paleness of her face, and in the depths of her brown eyes a secret excitement glowed.

Abruptly she turned away. Tomorrow she would be gone from here. This incident would soon be over and forgotten. That was all it was, an incident. An accident—stupid, but not harmful. Annoying, but not harmful . . .

Sleep seemed impossible. The small nagging headache behind her eyes had grown steadily more persistent. She had hoped it would go away, but it had not.

Señor Castillo had said his bedroom was nearby, and it should be a simple thing to go and ask for something to relieve the pain; still, she did not dare. If she appeared at the door of his room now, when they should both be settling down for the night, he could hardly be blamed for jumping to the wrong conclusion. He had done so once already, and she did not, just now, feel equal to making the situation clear to him if he should react in the same manner. The imprint of his kiss seemed to linger on her mouth, an indelible reminder of the contemptuous regard in which he held the women who forced themselves on him.

She might have mentioned her headache to María, of course, though at the time it had not seemed worth the effort of overcoming both the woman's hostility and the language barrier. She had no one but herself to blame for the restless night she saw stretching before her.

And yet, the moment she closed her eyes, she felt herself floating in a gray void that grew gradually darker. She slept.

Pain, throbbing with the beat of her heart, pulsing like a current through her head, awakened her. The dim light of early morning sifting through the curtains revealed the furnishings of the French bedroom standing in ghostly splendor around her. Anne stared at them blankly, without recognition.

Then she remembered. She was in the house of Señor Ramón Carlos Castillo, an unwilling, and unwelcome, guest. She must get up, put on her clothes, and get ready to leave. The flight to Dallas might be an early one.

She started to raise herself on one elbow, then stopped as her head exploded with pain. Her vision blurred. Nausea rose in her throat, subsiding as she remained completely still. She closed her eyes tightly, opening them only when the throbbing had faded to a steady ache.

She could not stay here in bed doing nothing. It might be hours before someone came. She had to get up. Perhaps if she had some kind of medication she would be able to move about enough to dress herself and be ready to leave on time. In her pain-filled mind, that seemed more important than anything else. It was a goal to fasten her will and her strength upon.

By slow degrees she got out of bed and made her way, holding to the furniture, to the door. Surely, she reasoned as she paused after each movement, her appearance at the señor's door this morning could not be misunderstood. In any case, if he touched her, she would scream, she would not be able to help herself.

She unlocked the door with difficulty. The hall outside stretched dark except for a single pool of light cast by a hanging lantern onto the crimson, Arabesque hall runner. There did not appear to be another soul stirring in the house.

An instant later, Anne realized her mistake. A thin line of light was coming from beneath one of the doors just up the hall from her own. Taking a deep breath, she moved toward it.

A woman's voice answered her knock. Anne's relief was short-lived however, for the woman who opened the panel was not María. She was tall and slim, with aquiline features plus the self-possessed air and telltale lines of a woman in her late twenties or early thirties. Her black hair was parted in the center and drawn back into a knot of uncompromising severity on the nape of her neck. She wore a plain robe of fawn velvet that did nothing to relieve the sallowness of her complexion, and her thin-lipped mouth looked as though it had never relaxed into a smile. Her shallow brown eyes widened in shock at the sight of Anne, then an unbecoming flush of anger surged to her hairline.

"Who are you? What are you doing here?" she demanded.

"I'm Anne Matthews. I came with Señor Castillo," Anne answered the questions painstakingly. "Do you have an aspirin—anything for pain? I have a terrible headache."

"What do you mean, you came with Señor Castillo? I demand an explanation!"

Anne put her hand to her head. The shrill timbre of the woman's voice seemed to slice into her brain. "On the plane—from Dallas," she replied in a low murmur.

"From Dallas!" The woman bit her lip. "You—you are perhaps a new secretary Ramón has hired for his American operations?"

Anne shook her head. "Please . . ."

"Then I am waiting for you to explain what you are doing here, and why you are wearing the night gown of Ramón's sister, Estela?" the woman exclaimed, holding her hands together at her waist, her mouth tight with disapproval as she surveyed the soft curves of Anne's breasts just visible through the lace bodice of the gown in the light falling from inside the room.

Anne's patience and endurance was wearing thin. "I am here because Señor Castillo insisted that I stay with him. As for the gown, I had nothing to wear."

"So Señor Castillo insisted, did he?" the woman sneered. "I should think you might call him by his given name then, considering . . ."

"I don't know what you mean," Anne began.

"You should be very proud," the other woman rushed on. "Yes, proud that you have caused Ramón Castillo to alter the principles of a lifetime for your sake."

From the corner of her eye, Anne was aware of the approach of a black-garbed figure. It was the housekeeper, María, hastening in their direction, making futile quieting motions with her hands. Inside the door, the other woman was not aware of her advance, or of the appearance in the hall from another room of a frail older woman wrapped in a lace-edged dressing gown.

"I only hope," the black-haired woman continued in her tirade, "that you do not live to regret dragging Ramón down to your level, or see the day when he will despise you for it."

"It isn't like that," Anne tried to say, though her voice was so weak she doubted the other woman heard her.

She did however. "Isn't it? Isn't it indeed? You needn't deny it. If you were not his woman, his traveling companion, why would Ramón allow you to invade the privacy of his plane, off-limits to his own relatives? Why would he bring you into his home and dress you in his sister's wardrobe? Tell me that! Explain it to me. I am waiting."

"Why, indeed, Irene?" The question came in the

faintly querulous voice of an elderly woman in a temper. "It may be," she went on, "that I have more faith in my grandson than you, but it appears to me there is another explanation."

"Tía Isabel!" the thin woman identified as Irene cried, stepping forward into the hall, brushing both Anne and the nurse aside. "What are you doing out of bed?"

"You know I seldom sleep this time of morning. I came to see what the disturbance was, and here I find you abusing a guest. What kind of conduct is this, I ask you? You take too much on yourself."

Irene picked up one of the small hands of the elderly woman, caressing the fine, parchment-colored skin. "This woman has come with Ramón," she explained in a soothing tone. "In my hurt and anger that he should bring such disgrace to this house I may have let my temper have too free a rein. Forgive me."

With a soft mutter of distress, the housekeeper moved closer to the old woman, but her mistress waved her to one side.

"And what," Doña Isabel asked, "has led you to believe that Ramón would disgrace his home? Have you proof of this extraordinary statement?"

Flinging out her hand in Anne's direction, Irene declared, "There is your proof."

The elderly woman lifted fine old eyes to Anne's pale face. Her aristocratic features were lined with age, but there could be no doubt this was Señor Castillo's grandmother. Anne, holding to her composure by sheer willpower, returned the searching regard of the older woman for long moments. She thought, as the wise old eyes turned away, that something like warmth had risen in their depths.

"I see only an attractive young woman who looks far from well," Doña Isabell announced in firm tones.

"Por favor, señora," the housekeeper pleaded, adding

what had the sound of a warning admonition in her native tongue. When no one paid the slightest attention to her, she eased away down the hall.

"Tía Isabel, must I put into words what I suspect?" Irene asked.

"I am afraid you must," the old woman told her without the least sign of understanding.

"This woman, I fear she is the—the mistress, the kept woman, of Ramón."

"That is a vicious thing to say of a young woman who is my grandson's guest. I would not have thought it of you. There is a much more likely explanation that occurs to me."

Irene stiffened as at the expectation of a blow. "And that is?"

"That she is the novia, the—how do you say?—fiancée of Ramón, whom he has brought to me so that I might come to know her, and to bless their union." Lifting her voice, she went on, "Is that not right, Ramón?"

Señor Castillo, with María trotting at his heels, came striding down the hall, tying the belt of his robe as he walked. That he was in a rage was plain from the frown between his eyes, and yet he checked at his grandmother's words, his dark gaze holding hers as he came on more slowly. He took her hand in a casual gesture of support.

"Should you be out of bed, Abuelita?" he asked quietly.

"I was awake early, as usual, and heard Irene browbeating this young woman. How could I not intervene?"

"Browbeating?" Irene exclaimed. She would have said more had Ramón Castillo not raised his hand in an imperious command for silence.

"Browbeating," the old woman repeated with great firmness. "She was being unspeakably rude to her, hint-ing at a clandestine relationship carried on brazenly beneath this roof. I felt compelled to tell her such was not, could not be, the case. That I was certain, in fact, that your explanation for the presence of so attractive a young woman must be quite otherwise."

Ramón Castillo made no reply. A furrow of concentration between his brows, he stared at his grandmother.

Irene broke the silence. "Is it true? Is she your fiancée?"

"This is neither the time nor the place to discuss such things," he said abruptly, flicking a quick glance in Anne's direction. As they talked, Anne had moved back slightly to lean against the wall. Noticing her wan appearance, Señor Castillo's frown deepened.

"I see," Irene breathed. "You do not deny it. How dare you? How dare you? We had an understanding."

It was the old woman who answered. "Dare, Irene? Why should he not? Don't, please, carry on like a— like a Victorian novel. This is the twentieth century. Your father and my son, Ramón's father, may have spoken of a marriage between you when you were both in your cradles, but the only understanding was in your own mind."

María, hovering anxiously, put her hand on the elderly woman's arm. "Doña Isabel," she pleaded.

Irene threw up her head. "Ramón, will you let your grandmother speak for you?"

The señor lifted a brow. "I doubt that I could better what she has said."

An angry spot of color appeared on the woman's cheekbones as she turned to Doña Isabel. "I knew that you resented me. I did not know that you had poisoned Ramón's mind against me as well. All right. I will not stay here and be insulted. I will go, now, at once! Perhaps then you will be happy. But when this weak American with her pale face and her headaches in the middle of the night has taken from both of you all you have to give and then gone on her way, I hope that you will think of me, and know what you threw away."

Spitting the last words at them, she whirled back into her bedroom and slammed the door.

The old woman sighed, her shoulders sagging. "I might have known she would take it like that," she said, half to herself.

"Yes, you might," her grandson replied. "Am I to take it that was not your object?"

"No," Doña Isabel answered, a reluctant smile twitching at her mouth. "You were always too perceptive, Ramón."

He ignored the last. "You look well," he said. "It would seem quarreling is good for you."

"There is a certain truth in that. I was never so ill as to send for you, however. That was Irene's doing. I grew so tired of her meddling with my routine, re-arranging the household to suit herself, and telling me everyday that I look more ill than the day before that I took to my bed and refused to see either her or the doctor she had called in place of my own family physician. She panicked, I think. Never have I been so angry as when I heard she had sent for you, taking you away from your business concerns for nothing. If you want her back, I will apologize, of course, but otherwise, no."

"I do not consider your well-being nothing. I had no idea that I was leaving you in such bad hands," her grandson said seriously.

"I have tried to tell you, though I must admit she has grown worse this last time you were away. But never mind that. You are sure you are not angry? You have no regrets?"

Anne thought he hesitated a moment before he leaned forward to kiss the soft crepe skin of Doña Isabel's cheek. "None, so long as you are happy."

"And this child here?" she said, indicating Anne. "I think something was said of a headache, and indeed, she doesn't look at all well."

As they all three turned to face her, Anne tried to smile. She felt oddly embarrassed, as though she had been watching a play and the actors had suddenly asked her to come on stage. There was a nimbus of light around the old lady's white hair and also around Señor Castillo's dark, arrogant head. The housekeeper seemed to be peering at her with less animosity than she had previously shown. "I'm sorry," Anne whispered. "I didn't mean to be so much trouble. I only wanted something for my headache."

"Don Ramón . . ."

Anne heard the housekeeper's warning accents; then, though she had not been aware that she was falling, she felt herself caught up and swung high against a man's chest. She was carried a short way, then placed on the yielding softness of a mattress. When she opened her eyes, she saw through the blur of tears of pain, the rose-colored hangings of her bed. Señor Castillo was a wavering shape beside the bed. Before she could gather her thoughts to speak, he was gone.

He returned almost immediately. With an arm behind her back, he helped her to sit up. He shook out a capsule from a small bottle and put it into her hand, then gave her a glass of water. When she had taken the capsule, she sank back down on the pillows and closed her eyes. After a moment, she felt the light touch of a sheet and blanket being tucked around her.

"Thank you," she murmured. In the recesses of her mind, she realized the señor still stood beside the bed staring down at her. She moved restlessly, disturbed by something she did not understand in his silence. A long moment later she heard his footsteps receding. The door closed behind him.

Chapter 3

Sleep. She wanted the drifting unconsciousness to go on forever, and yet she wanted also to awaken. She could not quite achieve either state. Vaguely, she knew when a short, dapper Mexican with a Vandyke beard came to examine her. His probing fingers at her temple made her head start to pound once more. The capsule he gave her was much like the one Señor Castillo had brought to her, and had much the same effect. She drank some beef bouillon through a straw at the insistence of the Spanish nurse, but went back to sleep before she could manage to eat the crackers that came with it. Once, she opened her eyes to see the señor silhouetted against the moonlight beyond her window, staring out in a brooding absorption. When she looked again, he was gone. A young girl she thought of as a maid flitted in and out of the room at odd hours, always trying to be quiet, never quite succeeding. It was she who found Anne awake at last.

"Buenas Dias," she said, a smile spreading over her round face. "Good morning. Is that not right?"

With a slow nod, Anne returned the greeting. The movement brought no pain. Her headache was gone.

Seeing her sudden smile, the maid said. "You are better this morning, no? The doctor, he say you can get up if you feel like it."

"What time is it?" Anne asked, nudged by a vague feeling that it was important.

"It is after eight o'clock in the morning, señorita. You have had a good sleep?"

The girl's laugh was infectious. Anne found herself smiling before she realized that the joke was on her.

"How—how long have I been here?" she asked, a shade of anxiety in her voice.

"It is not to worry, señorita," the maid replied soothingly. "It is only two days."

Two days! Anne sat up straight in bed. "And today is—"

"Monday, señorita."

"It can't be," she cried in horror; still, even as she said it, she knew there was no mistake. What in the world would Judy and Iva and Joe be thinking? They would have a missing-person bulletin out for her at the very least, especially if they found Judy's car deserted at the airport. Throwing back the sheet, she swung her legs off the bed.

"Wait, señorita, let me help you," the maid exclaimed, hurrying around the bed. "There is no need for such haste. I will bring your coffee, and perhaps you will take breakfast in bed, no?"

"No," Anne answered. "I have to get up and get dressed, right now. I have to speak to Señor Castillo. Where are my clothes?"

"They have been cleaned and pressed, and I, Carmelita, hung them away in the wardrobe with my own hands. But, señorita, you will make yourself ill again if you get up too soon. Please to have breakfast slowly in bed, then I will run your bath and lay out your clothes. That is the way. Besides, Don Ramón has not left his room to go down to the patio for breakfast, and he sees no one before then. For my life I would not disturb him, not me!"

Daunted by such a heartfelt declaration, Anne

paused. After a moment, she asked, "What about after breakfast?"

"That would be much better. While you are making yourself ready I will speak to Pedro, Don Ramón's secretary, and see what may be arranged."

Irritation with such formality touched Anne, then receded. "Thank you," she replied.

The light of the sun was blinding after the dim interior of the house. Anne stood for a moment in the doorway to let her eyes adjust. The patio, including the dim recess under the arched and columned loggia that encompassed it on four sides, was large. It was paved with gray stone except for a circle of yellow and blue geometric tiles that made a base for a sparkling fountain. Orange trees lifted their glossy branches to shade one corner. Under the loggia hung baskets of enormous ferns and flowering begonias. Fine green moss grew between the cracks of the floor. Hardy ferns lined the edge of the loggia, and placed at intervals were large terra-cotta pots filled with cascades of white petunias growing around the bases of red geraniums. Through an arched opening in the wall closed by an iron grill could be seen an expanse of the garden and the wall that bounded the property. Roses and sweet peas clambered over the wall, a pink and magenta and rose mass of fragrance with bees drunkenly picking and choosing among them.

Glancing up from his paper, Señor Castillo caught sight of her hovering there under the arcade. He rose to his feet at once, tossing aside the paper, and held out a chair for her at the glass-topped wrought-iron table where he had been sitting.

"Coffee?" he asked as he resumed his place. A coffee service of heavy, polished silver sat before him on a tray though all evidence of his breakfast had been removed. Since it would give her something to do with her hands, Anne agreed. He poured it out and, without consulting her, added sugar before passing the cup to her.

"You are rested?" he asked, his narrowed gaze on the pale fragility of her face as he sat back with his own cup.

"Yes, perfectly," she answered, "though I must apologize for the trouble I have caused."

"It was nothing."

"I'm sure it was awkward for you. I—I would like to thank you for taking care of me." It was difficult to go on in the face of his apparent indifference, but she had to have his cooperation. It might be days before she could untangle the mess she was in and return home without his help. "I cannot quite remember, but it seems I must have told you that I have friends, my employers and my roommate, who will be worried about me. Do you know—is there some way I could get in touch with them and let them know I am all right?"

"Certainly. The telephone is available whenever you would like to use it. However, you need be in no hurry to contact your employers. I have spoken to them already. They know where you are and the circumstances, and will not expect to hear from you any time soon. It is more than likely that your roommate will learn of your whereabouts from them when you don't turn up, don't you think?"

"You—you called Metcalf's about me?" As Anne set her coffee cup on the table it clattered a little in the saucer.

"From the plane," he admitted with the faintest flicker of a smile. "You would not tell me your name, if you remember, and I had to know it, along with a number of other particulars, in order to persuade the authorities to let you into the country."

"Then you are convinced that I came to be on your

plane as I said?" she asked, unable to resist pursuing this sore point.

"Let us say I am convinced you are employed with Metcalf Caterers. For the rest . . ." He shrugged.

Anne stared at his shuttered expression in frustration. The guard, that was it. Señor Castillo still considered that, discovering herself on his plane with the guard who had seen her go on board out of the way, she had taken advantage of the situation to bring herself to his notice. It was infuriating, but the only thing she could do about it was to take herself off as quickly as possible.

Taking a deep breath for composure, she said, "Then you will be happy to see me go. If you will arrange my flight as you suggested the night we arrived, I won't trespass on your hospitality any longer."

A frown of concentration between his eyes, he stared past her into the shadows under the loggia. Propping his elbow on the arm of his chair, he pulled at his lower lip. Abruptly, he brought his hand down. His dark, intense gaze on her face, he asked, "Why do you want to go?"

"Why?" she repeated, at a loss.

"You have no family, no close man friend. What is there to hold you in Dallas? Why is it necessary for you to return?"

"I have friends, acquaintances, people I have known all my life. It's my home. There is my job—"

"Friends can be made in other places. As for the job, there is one here for you."

"Here, in Mexico?"

"Here, in my home."

For a moment she was tempted. To stay in Mexico, to see more of the country and its people, would be a lovely thing. It was the only way to really get to know another land. But to be alone in that land, away from everything known and familiar? No. She did not quite have the courage.

"I'm sorry," she began.

"But you have not heard what your position will be," he interrupted, a dry note in his voice. "Aren't you being a bit hasty?"

"I don't see that it matters," Anne said defensively.

"No? What I am offering you, Anne Matthews, is the position, the paid, temporary position—let me make that clear—of my fiancée. Who knows? There is always the possibility, if you play your cards right, that the position might become permanent."

Anger impelled Anne to her feet. With one hand resting on the table, she stared at him, aware of a pulse behind her eyes, a warning that her headache would return if she allowed herself to be upset much further. "If this is your idea of a joke—"

"Not at all. I am perfectly serious," he answered without moving.

"Why? I see no reason for you to go to such lengths to acquire a fiancée. I'm sure," she added with the most telling of deadpan sarcasm, "that you must know dozens of women who would be only too delighted to take the position for nothing."

A muscle tightened in his jaw, but he did not raise his voice. "Unfortunately you are the one my grandmother identified to Irene as my future wife. The ploy, mistaken though it was, was helpful in ridding my house of a woman who had become, in fact, one of the kind of entanglements I have been trying to avoid for years. The situation is complicated by the added fact that she is my distant cousin and I am, in a sense, her guardian until her marriage. Our fathers were not only related, they were close friends. They stood godfather to each other's children and executors to each other's wills. They did not, you perceive, plan also to die together, but they did, in a boating accident."

The conventional response was automatic. Señor Castillo disregarded it.

"I did not tell you these things for sympathy. I only want you to understand my position. My first concern in this matter is to see that my grandmother is not disturbed by Irene again. The best way to assure that is to have her go on thinking I am engaged to another woman."

There was an obvious flaw in that plan; still, Anne saw no need to point it out to him since she had no intention of agreeing to it.

"My second thought," the señor went on, "is to relieve my grandmother's mind concerning your presence—the seed of doubt Irene planted as to our relationship was a destructive one, and I will not have Abuelita worrying over it. She was brought up in an age of strict moral standards and cannot easily forgive anyone she thinks may have failed to meet them. It has been a long time since she has felt it necessary to pray over me, and I don't intend for it to happen again."

That was understandable, even laudable, though privately Anne considered it a useless precaution. She had detected no doubt in Doña Isabel's manner toward her grandson.

"My third reason you are already familiar with, and I see little reason to give you the opportunity to level the charge of conceit at me again," he continued with a slight smile. "There may be among my friends a woman who would be glad to assist me, but I'm afraid her price would be too high to make the game worth the candle."

"Your freedom," Anne ventured.

"Exactly."

"Aren't you afraid that my price might be just as high?" she asked, a curious light in her brown eyes.

His answer was brief. "With you I am forewarned."

"Then," she said gently, "there is little reason for me to do as you wish, is there?"

She had silenced him. Still, the expression on his face as he watched her swing around and walk back into the house made her uneasy. What would he do now? Would he make the arrangements for her flight as she had asked, or would he try again to persuade her. She had no choice but to wait and see.

"Señorita?"

The quiet call came with a knock on the bedroom door. Anne, intrigued by the stealthiness of that soft summons, moved to answer it at once.

The maid Carmelita stood outside. "Pardon señorita, but Doña Isabel wishes to speak with you if it is convenient," she said, her round face flushed as she darted a glance up and down the hallway.

Doña Isabel. Anne had a hazy memory of the white-haired old woman. Señor Castillo's grandmother. Much of what had occurred on the night she arrived had become clearer in her mind since her talk with the señor, but she could not recall the exact part Doña Isabel had played. She was supposed to be ill, very nearly on her deathbed, or so Anne had thought, and yet she had been strong enough to put Irene in her place.

The secretive attitude of the maid was puzzling too. Why should Doña Isabel not speak to her grandson's guest if she wished? Who would care, and why? The best way to find out was to speak to the old woman.

Carmelita led Anne down the hall to the far end where she tapped on a door and pushed it open. Standing to one side, she held the door for Anne then went out, closing it gently behind her. The housekeeper, who seemed to serve also as nurse-companion, stood beside the slight figure in the bed. In her hand she held a tray on which the invalid had just placed a small glass bearing the telltale purple stain of grape

juice. At some unseen signal, she smiled at Anne and
followed the maid from the room.

"Señorita Matthews, I am so glad you could give me
a moment of your time. I was afraid you would be too
busy with your preparations to leave us. Come in,
child, come in. There is no need to stand on ceremony.
Take a chair, here beside the bed so I can see you."

Doña Isabel sat propped against lace-edged pillows in
a canopied bed of mammoth proportions. Bed curtains
of yellow muslin under gold velvet hung from the
heavy mahogany frame. The same materials were
drawn back from a series of arched windows that
looked down into the central patio, letting in a flood of
golden sunlight. In the warm glow, the old lady, sitting
up in the bed in a lavender bed jacket with her long
hair hanging in a silver plait over her shoulder, seemed
vividly alive.

Anne's smile as she seated herself on the slipper
chair covered in cream brocade was rueful. "I hate to
admit it, but I have no preparations to make at this
moment. I'm not sure I know quite what to do."

"I hope you will allow yourself to be guided by my
grandson," the old woman said, an odd inflection in
her voice.

Passing over the suggestion, Anne went on. "In any
case, I am glad to be able to come and thank you for
intervening the other night, and to be certain that you
were—that you did not—"

"That I did not collapse after the ordeal? No, no,
my dear, though it is kind of you to be concerned. I
am not on my last legs, I assure you, whatever you may
have been led to believe."

"I didn't mean that exactly," Anne tried to explain.

"No? I can't think why not. I'm sure you had every
reason to expect it. And that is one of the things I
wanted to talk to you about, though I cannot do so
without touching on your relationship with my grand-

son, something I think you are reluctant to discuss. Am I correct?"

"There is no relationship between us to discuss," Anne said, returning Doña Isabel's gaze frankly.

"Even though he asked you to be his fiancée?" the old lady asked in quiet disbelief. Then, seeing the questioning look on Anne's face, she went on. "I have ways of knowing what is going on in this house. I have lived here all my life, known the servants, most of them, since they were children. If Ramón does not want me to know of his affairs, he should choose a more secluded place for his interviews than an open patio where the gardeners are working."

Anne smiled at her droll expression. "Your grandson offered to pay me to pretend to be his fiancée, a different thing entirely."

Doña Isabel frowned. "But not something he would ask of a complete stranger, or a woman in whom he had no interest?"

"Even if he did wish to become personally involved with the woman?" Anne suggested.

The old lady folded her hands across the sheet that covered her to the waist. "I can see I am going to have to ask you to tell me the complete story. I hope," she continued with a flickering smile that reminded Anne of her grandson, "that you are not going to disappoint me."

It was not possible, of course. With a shake of her head, Anne began her story.

When she had finished, Doña Isabel nodded. "I begin to see. I think I understand his motives, even if I can't approve of his methods. In my attempt to defend his good name, I represented you to Irene as someone dear to him, and he is trying to keep me from looking the fool. It is just like him."

"I don't see how it can matter what was said in the privacy of his home," Anne objected.

"You do not know Irene. She has gone to an apartment in the center of the city. I imagine she has lost no time in acquainting her circle of friends with the cruel way in which she was treated; encouraged to think herself the chosen bride of Ramón, only to be ousted in the middle of the night in favor of a stranger, and a norteamericano at that! It will make an affecting enough tale without her being able to add the fact that you, my dear, were no more than a—a passing fancy, brought into his house under the same roof as his grandmother who is on her deathbed."

"I cannot believe anyone would accept her word for what took place against your grandson's, or that he would care if they did."

"Envy makes people credulous where the rich and powerful are concerned. They would believe it. As for Ramón's being concerned, no, not for himself. Still, he is a businessman with many interests, many people large and small who depend on him. Where there is great responsibility, there must also be great integrity. In Mexico, the trust given a man depends to a large extent on that old-fashioned concept, his honor."

"But—" Anne began.

"Naturally, he could go to his associates and say that Irene lies, but she is his cousin. Such a course would not only be against his principles, it would be against the interests of the family. To us, this still means something. So, would it not be better to make what Irene thinks to be so true indeed, at least for a short time? There is much to be gained, and little to lose. You will be seen a few times with Ramón, and soon his friends will be saying they do not blame him for preferring a lovely creature like you to his sour cousin. For yourself, you will have a nice holiday for two weeks—three—a month; then there will be a small quarrel in public with Ramón and you will return home somewhat richer than when you came."

The old lady made everything seem so logical, so simple. As her soft voice went on and on, Anne could feel her resolve weakening. "But I don't even like your grandson," she protested.

"Don't you?" The old woman tilted her head to one side. "Why not? He is thought to be a most attractive man, even without the undoubted allure of his money."

"He still thinks I deliberately stayed on his plane in order to bring myself to his attention."

"Tiresome of him, but going away will not convince him otherwise, nor will it give you satisfaction. Only by staying can you be revenged on him. It will be within your power to make him suffer, just a little you understand, for his attitude."

"I don't want to make him suffer," Anne said rather desperately.

"Don't you? Then you are more forgiving than I would be in your place," Señor Castillo's grandmother said.

"He—he could have abandoned me when we reached Mexico City," Anne pointed out in an attempt to be fair.

"A Castillo? Never," Doña Isabel declared. "Especially not a woman of your attractions."

"I'm not that attractive," Anne said, as mutinously as if it made a difference to what the elderly woman was suggesting.

"Because you refuse to allow yourself to be. You could be truly beautiful with the right clothes, the right attention. It would be great fun to bring about the transformation. To see my grandson's fiancée creditably established would also be sufficient reason for me to leave my bed and go out and about again. You see, my motives are not entirely unselfish."

Turning her head in a wary gesture, Anne asked, "Meaning?"

"Meaning," Doña Isabel answered slowly, "that I

will do anything to keep Irene from returning to this house. She is the grandchild of my eldest sister, long dead, but I cannot bear to have her near me, nor does she feel any affection for me, for all of her extravagant claims otherwise. To her, I was no more than an excuse to force her way into Ramón's company when he showed no inclination to seek hers. Ramón was fooled by her pretense of devotion and installed her as my companion over my protests. It was done, no doubt, for my own good, but I have not yet forgiven him for it. Lately she had grown sure of her position, sure that she could manipulate me, and Ramón, as she saw fit. She made it plain that she considered me an encumbrance she would be rid of as soon as she and Ramón were wed. For the sake of my health, of course, I would be shuttled into a very comfortable, very expensive home for the aged. Toward this end, she made a great display of my infirmities, calling attention to every lapse of memory in the most sorrowful tones, arranging the menus so I was fed gruel and milk and toast and stewed fruit suited to my invalid condition, wrapping me up in shawls and blankets until I almost suffocated from the heat. She cautioned me every time I put my foot to the floor, pushed a footstool at me every time I sat down, handed me my glasses when I could well put my hand on them, fussed about drafts and my favorite chocolate candy and the amount of coffee I enjoyed, and the fatal effects of colds and insects bites and evening air until I was ready to pass away in an apoplexy from sheer irritation of the nerves."

The old woman took a deep breath, her eyes flashing. "I was driven to staying in my room, curtailing my visits for fear of what she would do in my absence, and my visitors for fear of what she would say to them behind my back. Ramón was away so much he thought my retreat from physical causes. That being so, he did not like to leave me alone with only the servants when he was absent. The complaints I had to make of Irene sounded to his ears like attentions for which I should have been grateful. But the last straw came when she took it upon herself to summon Ramón simply because I closed my door to her, seeing only my own María, whom I have known all my life. I heard her tell that quack of a doctor she sent for that I was indulging in a childish fit."

Doña Isabel actually snorted, a flush of anger pink across the parchment of her cheeks. "Well, I had enough wits about me to put such a menace from me, but I cannot rest until I am certain there is no chance of her return."

"Surely if you explained to your grandson as you have to me he will understand?" Anne told her, firmly resisting the impulse to make her tone soft and soothing.

"He will not listen. She has poisoned his mind until he sees me as an invalid to be pampered with grape juice and protected from all things. He does it from his great love for me, this I understand, but it makes me afraid that his love will cause him to wrap me up and put me away like a precious toy grown too fragile to play with. He needs someone else to love, someone else to distract his mind, but not, please God, Irene. If there is some small thing I can do to stall off that calamity, I will. Won't you help me, señorita? Won't you please say you will help me?"

There could be only one answer to such an impassioned plea. "I would like to, Señora Castillo, though I don't see what you hope to gain by this masquerade when it will last such a short while."

"Time. I will gain time in which to prove myself as sane and well as anyone of my age. Time to show him I do not need a watchdog. Time is always an ally.

Much can happen if there is time. . . ." A faraway look had crept into Doña Isabel's eyes.

Gently Anne said, "Yes, I see what you mean."

"Then, you will do as Ramón has suggested?" the old woman asked, clasping her fingers together. "You will explain to him that you have changed your mind and now agree?"

"Yes, I suppose so," she said. It was not something she looked foreward to doing.

"It would be well to tell him as soon as possible, before he has had a chance to reconsider or to see to the details of your flight back to the United States."

"You wouldn't like to tell him, I suppose?" Anne asked with a wry smile.

"I could," Doña Isabel answered slowly, "but I do not think it would be best. As I said, I believe I am involved in Ramón's reasons for his proposal to you. I am not, you remember, to know this engagement is not real. Naturally, you will accept my congratulations when the time comes without any indication of this little talk we have had."

"Yes, I understand," Anne agreed, though privately she was already beginning to wonder what she had let herself in for.

She was not left long in doubt. The moment she left Doña Isabel's room, Carmelita seized upon her. "Señorita, you must hurry. Don Ramón is waiting for you in his library—has been for this half-hour while the chauffeur sits in the car outside the door."

Anne felt a tightening in the pit of her stomach. "Why didn't you come for me?"

Smiling over her shoulder, Carmelita said, "María has told me Don Ramón has asked you to be his novia. It is not good for a woman to run when the man she is to marry calls. It spoils him as a husband, no?"

It was impossible to explain. Anne only shook her

head, hoping that Señor Castillo shared Carmelita's attitude.

The library was a surprising room, more modern than Spanish colonial in character. It was fitted out like an office with an enormous desk fronting a matching chair in green leather, a dictating machine, typewriter, and double row of file cabinets. There were bookshelves stretching to the ceiling with the bright covers of American editions among the somber leather-bound volumes. On the wall facing the door was a mural in vivid turquoise, cream, black, tan, and terra-cotta. Seated at the desk in front of the colorful painting, Señor Castillo seemed almost a part of the parade of bronze Aztec warriors depicted in a geometric swirl of ancient symbols amid the small figures of houses, horses, scorpions, and angels.

"So," he said, tossing aside a sheaf of papers and waving her to a chair, "you did not run away."

"No," she replied when it seemed he expected her to comment.

"They were so long in finding you that I was beginning to think you had taken fright and run screaming to the American embassy."

The suggestion was not very flattering. Her voice was cool as she answered, "As you can see, I am still here."

He was silent, as if waiting for her explanation for keeping him waiting. Remembering Doña Isabel's admontion that it would be unwise to let him know they had been talking, she was just as silent. She even felt a perverse satisfaction in thewarting him. It was short-lived, however.

"I hope," he said at last, "that you have been using the time to reconsider your answer to my offer."

Now was the time to agree. Here was the opportunity. "I have been thinking about it, yes."

"Conclusively?"

When she did not answer at once, a grim expression

appeared about his mouth. Before she could frame a reply, he spoke again.

"I have tried persuasion. I have tried bribery. I think now the time has come to use blackmail."

The words of acquiesence she had been about to speak left her. "Meaning?" she asked in a voice that sounded thin to her own ears.

"The catering firm of Metcalf's is a fine organization, but a small one. I wonder what the effect would be upon its finances if I were to withdraw my account?"

Anne stared at him. "You wouldn't."

"You think not? There is one way to be certain that I do not."

"I thought you were a man of—of honor," she said slowly.

The blood receded from his face. There was a dark glitter in his eyes and his voice was soft as he answered. "Instead, you find that I am a man who likes to have his own way. You would do well to remember it."

"I will try," she said, "since it seems I must. I will do as you ask, but only for two weeks. After that, you will have to make some other arrangement."

"We will see," was his only reply to her ultimatum. It was not completely satisfactory.

Possibly her quick agreement took him by surprise, for he seemed at something of a loss, drumming his fingers on the desk, staring hard at a leather-encased calendar before turning his attention back to her.

"Would you like to see about the time away from Metcalf's or shall I?" he asked abruptly.

"If you don't mind, I would like to speak to Iva Metcalf personally."

"Why should I mind?" he said irritably. "I presume you would like to discuss your wardrobe with this roommate of yours also, though it would be more economical, probably, to buy what you need here. However, I will leave that to you. The telephone is at your disposal. Also, Pedro, my secretary, will be available this morning if you need to make some arrangement to fly your baggage here—anything else will be too slow to be helpful. You will need summer-weight clothing, remember, and evening wear."

"Evening wear?" she queried in surprise. The only thing suitable for evening in her closet at home was a long velvet skirt she had bought on impulse at a sale and never worn.

"Don't trouble yourself over it," he said, making a note at the same time on a pad before him. "Is there anything else you would like to know?"

"You intend to make this engagement public?" Something Doña Isabel had said had indicated that it might be so, but Anne had somehow doubted it.

"Yes, of course, Why not?"

Anne shook her head helplessly. "Señor Castillo, don't you think this is carrying things too far?"

"Ramón. You must learn to call me Ramón if you are to be convincing as my fiancée," he reproved her as he got to his feet and moved around the end of the desk to lean against it, standing over her. "And, no, I don't think it is. Half-measures never serve."

"But, señor—"

"Ramón," he insisted.

"I'm sorry. I can't seem to think of you in that way," she said, her head coming up sharply in an instant reaction to the trace of command in his tone.

"Perhaps this will help you," he said, and bending over her, captured her upturned lips with his own.

An odd warmth stole along her veins, sapping her strength. The sudden play of something like flame along her mouth made her draw in her breath sharply. Smooth, sensuous, his lips held her poised on the brink of an unknown pleasure; then abruptly, he raised his head. His eyes, dark and unreadable, burned into hers for an instant before his lashes came down to shield his expression.

A lower timbre than usual in his voice, he said, "Between a man and woman who are to be married there should be an impression of intimacy. I don't believe it will be hard to counterfeit, given a little practice."

Anne swallowed, her gaze dropping to the sheen of his silk shirt collar. "I expect not," she murmured, and wandered at the sense of anticipation she felt drawing as tightly as a wire within herself. Whether it was composed of dread or excitement, she could not say.

Chapter 4

The day passed slowly. Anne spent the remainder of the morning trying to get in touch with Judy and talking to Iva Metcalf on the phone. There was no difficulty in getting a two-week absence from the catering firm. Iva demanded to know what Anne thought she was up to, but there was no anger in her voice, only an intrigued curiosity.

"It's the most romantic thing I ever heard of," she said, her voice coming clear and sane over the wire. "You could have knocked me over with the proverbial feather when we heard from Señor Castillo that you were with him on his plane. But you will be careful, won't you, Anne? I don't know what you think you're doing—and I'm not asking—you're a big girl now, and I don't have any right to play mother hen. Still, you head for home quick if things get too rough down there. You've got a week's salary coming and I'm sending it along, just in case. You never know when a little extra might come in handy."

Anne thanked her, and after promising to see to it that Judy got her message, or herself go over and pack the things Anne needed, Iva hung up. Talking with her disturbed Anne, however. Iva represented the normal, everyday routine. Before speaking to her, the position she was undertaking had seemed unusual, but not unreasonable. Afterward, it appeared fantastic, if not downright foolhardy.

During the afternoon she walked for a time in the garden, enjoying the warmth and the scent of the flowers. Beneath the shade of a strange tree that reminded her of a cypress she discovered a chaise of wrought iron fitted with cushions. She sat down and leaned back, lulled by the soft caress of a breeze on her face. For a long time she lay in drowzy content, not really asleep, yet not awake. It was there that Carmelita found her.

An excited light shone in the maid's round black eyes. In her arms she carried a dress box while she held an envelope between the fingers of one hand. "There you are, señorita," she exclaimed. "I have been looking for you everywhere. This box, she come for you by messenger, and there is a note also, from Don Ramón, I think."

There was indeed. The heavy cream-colored notepaper crackled under Anne's fingers. The slashing, upright letters in black ink were instantly recognizable as the kind of handwriting she would expect of Ramón, even without the initial with which he had signed the short message. There would be guests for dinner, she read, Ramón's sister and her husband, and also a business associate and his wife. The occasion would be formal. Since her own luggage would be unlikely to arrive in time, he had directed that a selection of suitable evening wear be sent to her. His own choice was the turquoise, but she was free to choose as she wished. If she should have scruples about taking the clothes, he invited her to consider his position. "I have no liking for the idea of appearing as King Cophetua to your beggar maid," he wrote.

How was she to take that last, she wondered? Was it intended as sarcasm, or as it sounded, a wry joke?

Carmelita, unabashedly reading the note over her shoulder, was in no doubt as to what should be done with the contents of the box. "Come, señorita," she urged. "Let us go and try on everything."

The temptation was too great to resist. When the box was emptied, three ensembles were spread out upon the bed. There was a dress with an old-fashioned look in blond lace, salmon muslin, and rust velvet, one in a softly flowing gold knit with a matching shawl trimmed in silk fringe, and last of all, there was the turquoise. Though definitely not mentioned in the note, there was also a small handbag containing a makeup kit, a complete set of underclothing, hosiery, and a pair of evening sandals in silver, gold, and tropical white. Everything was perfect, right down to the sandals. Giggling at her surprise, Carmelita admitted to providing Ramón with a list of her sizes taken from the clothes she had been wearing. There should be an air of intimacy between them, he had said. He was creating that with a vengeance.

The first two dresses were, as Ramón had said, suitable, but his final choice was also hers. The turquoise dress was simple in style with a softly draped neckline, cap sleeves, and a full skirt falling to the knee. It was the material that made it special, soft, lustrous tissue silk that shaded from deep sea blue to a gentle green with every movement. It was an enchanted dress, lending the wearer a mystic, illusive charm. Anne, staring at herself in the mirror, felt suddenly as though she had stepped inadvertently into a fairy tale, one it might be difficult to step back out of again.

It may have been that she and Carmelita took longer than she thought over trying the dresses, or maybe her dread of the evening was to blame, but the rest of the afternoon seemed to fly past. Dinner would be late, nearly two hours past the time she was accustomed to eating; still, before she realized it, it was time to begin to think about getting dressed.

Letting the water run hot and deep, she sprinkled the bath salts into the tub, breathing deeply of the smell reminiscent of gardenias. She had shampooed her hair that morning while she bathed, and now lacking pins to put it up out of the way, she wrapped her head turban fashion in one of the soft, thirsty towels, then stepped into the tub and lay back with a sigh. She tired easily, one of the effects of her concussion. That, she told herself, was the reason for her unaccustomed languor. Nevertheless, at this rate she would soon be spoiled. It would be fatally easy to grow used to having her every wish anticipated. It was with difficulty that she had convinced Carmelita that she was capable of dressing herself. She thought the friendly young maid had been disappointed that she was not wanted.

Anne was halfway down the stairs before she glanced up. At the foot stood Ramón, leaning with one elbow on the carved newel post, an odd expression on his face. Her nerves gave a tiny jerk, but she let no hint of her agitation show on her face. Head high, she continued to descend until she stood just above him.

"Chalchihuitlicue," he said, his tone registering satisfaction.

"What?" she asked, at a loss.

"Chalchihuitlicue," he repeated, "Our Lady of the Turquoise Skirt, an Aztec goddess who presided over lakes and rivers. She is always represented as a young girl of charm, beautifully dressed. I had not realized why the dress you are wearing attracted my attention until I saw you in it."

It was a skillful compliment, but compliments were something she was too unfamiliar with to be certain it was sincere. On the chance that it was, she thanked him in a low voice, then continued hurriedly, "But you shouldn't have gone to so much trouble and expense."

"I thought I had explained that," he said with an impatient gesture.

"I know," she answered, a slight frown between her eyes, "but that doesn't keep me from feeling uncomfortable about it."

"You feel more attractive in this dress, do you not?"

She had to admit she did.

"Then that is enough. If it is the morality of accepting such things that bothers you, put it out of your head. I am your fiancé, am I not? And I assure you, I require nothing of you in return."

Before she could recover her breath to reply, he turned sharply away. "Come, I would like a few minutes alone with you before we join the others."

He held the door of the library for her, closing it behind them as she passed through. Before moving to his desk, he indicated a chair for Anne, but she elected to stand.

From the desktop, he picked up a small, velvet-covered jeweler's box and, springing it open, held it out to her. Tucked into a bed of white satin was an oval-shaped diamond solitaire in a platinum setting.

When Anne looked from the ring to him without making a move to take it, Ramón asked, "Well, don't you like it?"

"It's lovely."

"Perhaps you expected something more elaborate? But your hands are so slender. Anything else would have looked clumsy, overpowering."

"Oh, no, it's not that. The ring is all any girl could wish for. I just—"

"There must be some outward sign of our engagement, you will agree to that? People will expect it."

"Yes."

"Then—it is the cost again?" he said, a hard look descending over his face.

She nodded.

"There is no necessity for you to feel that you must protest every cent spent on you merely because I suspected you of being interested in my money, my dear Anne. I am not impressed."

Anne felt a coldness settle around her heart. Without a word, she turned making swiftly for the door. He caught her before she had taken three steps, swinging her to face him, his hands on her forearms. His face was tight with rage. A threat seemed to hang in the air. Suddenly, Anne remembered Metcalf's and this man's power to harm Joe and Iva. Fear invaded her mind and she raised wide eyes to search Ramón's face.

He stared down at her, his fingers biting into her arms, a muscle corded along his jawline. Then with an abrupt movement, he released her.

"I'm sorry, Anne. I should not have said that. We will forget it, please."

The apology was so unexpected that she could make no answer. But neither did she object as he took the ring from the box and, picking up her hand, pushed it smoothly onto her finger. Her hand was cool in his warm grasp and he did not immediately let it go. He stared down at the pale oval of her face while tension grew between them. His hands moved to cup her elbows, drawing her close against him. She could feel the hardness of the planes of his chest and the muscles of his thighs.

"Anne," he said, a questioning note in his husky voice.

A knock, loud in the stillness, sounded on the door. Before they could move, the panel opened and a woman stuck her head into the room.

"May I come in? Whoops! Sorry, Ramón, but you shouldn't hide away with your fiancée when you have guests, especially a guest like me. You should have known I would chase you down, even in your sanctum."

"Anne, may I present my sister, Estela?" Ramón said dryly. With a show of reluctance that may or may not have been real, he dropped his hands from Anne and stepped to the door, ushering the small, vivacious, dark-haired girl into the room.

"It is a great pleasure to meet you," Estela said, casting a sparkling look at her brother. "We were beginning to despair of Ramón's ever succumbing to the lures of matrimony. I hope you will be happy here in Mexico with us."

Acknowledging the introduction, Anne thanked her. Ramón's sister, with her friendly smile and outspoken manner, was instantly likable. The evening before her began to look less of an ordeal.

Estela turned to Ramón. "I came looking for you for our grandmother's sake. She declares herself determined to come down for dinner and requires your arm down the stairs."

"Is she strong enough?" he asked quickly.

Estela smiled with quizzical humor. "She has always been strong enough to do what she really wishes."

"That doesn't make her well," Ramón pointed out.

"She is over seventy years old. What do you expect?"

He made no direct reply. "Come then, Anne, and let me introduce you to the others before I go up."

"Couldn't I help . . . with your grandmother?" Anne asked, holding back.

Surprise made his face blank for an instant before he replied, "I'm sure I can manage."

It had been a peculiar offer, perhaps, in view of Ramón's belief that she and his grandmother were near strangers. "Please," she said, making her smile warm and personal and just faintly entreating. "I would prefer to wait and meet the others only when I know you are near—in case I run into difficulties."

He took her point at once. His face cleared. "Of

course, *mi alma*. As you wish," he said, and encircling her waist with a casual gesture, led her out of the room under his sister's amused and approving gaze.

Doña Isabel was ready, sitting bolt upright in a straight-backed chair, in black lace, a magnificent parure of diamonds, and holding an ebony walking stick. A small prayer mantilla of black lace shot with silver covered the white silk of her hair. She acknowledged the formal presentation of her grandson's fiancée with a regal nod at variance with the kindling warmth in her eyes.

"You look charming this evening, my dear Anne. I may call you Anne?" the old lady said with an audacious smile for Anne alone. Receiving Anne's prompt permission, she went on. "May I compliment you on your evening frock? It is perfectly delightful, though I think— Ramón, would you be so kind as to fetch me my jewel casket?"

His black glance considered her for a moment, but she returned the look with such a serene expression that he moved to obey her.

"Ah, here is what I was looking for," the old woman said when the large satinwood box lined with green velvet was placed on her lap. From a small compartment she had taken a fine gold chain. Suspended from it was a lump of turquoise in the shape of a human heart. The stone veining on its surface had the look of gold tracery.

With an imperious gesture, Doña Isabel handed the gemstone to Ramón. "Here, put it on for Anne. It should go perfectly with what she is wearing. It was given to me many years ago by Ramón's grandfather, a token to go with a gown I had then much in the style of yours."

As he moved toward her with the pendant, Anne said in alarm, "I can't take this. It—it wouldn't be right."

"Nonsense," the old woman said, a satisfied look on her face as Ramón placed the chain around Anne's neck. "Aren't you going to be my grandson's wife?"

That question, and the limpid look of innocence that went with it, haunted Anne all evening. The turquoise gradually warming against her breast, she descended with Ramón and Doña Isabel to the living room, or *sala*, as it was called. Estela came forward to help her grandmother into a chair, and with her light chatter, helped to integrate Anne into the company.

Estela's husband was a quiet man several years her senior, a professor of history at the University of Mexico not far away. With his neat goatee, intelligent eyes, and briarwood pipe, he looked much like university professors everywhere. Ramón's business associate and his wife, Señor and Señora Martínez, were a middle-aged couple, both of them on the plump side. They held their glasses of sherry with self-conscious gentility, and, perhaps because they were nervous, reached often for the plate of hors d'oeuvres that sat on the table before them. With sympathy, Anne realized they were new to affluence and a little out of their depths socially. The fact helped her to feel not quite so uncomfortable herself. She was not alone in finding the Castillo family overwhelming.

Ramón did not leave her side. He pressed a small glass of sherry into her hand, then stood with his hand resting on the back of the chair in which she was seated. Together, they fielded the questions about where they had met and when, how long she would be visiting, and the probable date of their wedding. It was Ramón, however, using a skillful blend of fact, humor, and audacious imagination, who made their supposed romance sound a fantastic adventure leading inevitably to this moment, without revealing that it had begun less than a week before. Regardless of how good he was at half-truths, it was a relief when dinner was announced. Presenting an arm to each, Ramón took both Anne and his grandmother into the dining room.

Anne had somehow expected the meal, her first in the household that was not served to her on a tray, to consist of typical Mexican dishes only. Nothing could have been further from the truth. The menu was continental, with a predominance of French dishes in rich sauces, fresh vegetables simmered in butter, a salad, and for desert, a fruit ice followed by strong, hot coffee.

They were sitting over the demi-tasse cups when Estela, taking advantage of a pause, asked, "What do you all say to a performance of the Ballet Folklórico at the Palacio de Bellas Artes? This is something, Ramón, that Anne should see if she is to learn anything of the country she must make her own. It is a beautiful spectacle, I promise you, Anne, as well as being educational."

As Anne glanced uncertainly at Ramón, Estela went on. "Also there is Xochimilco—the floating gardens—Chapultepec Park and the castle, the pyramids at Teotihuacán—"

"Anne is not a tourist," her brother pointed out mildly. "There will be plenty of time for that sort of thing."

Turning to Anne, Estela said. "If I were you, I would watch him. If you let him he will do nothing but work, work, work, and you will soon find yourself a widow."

"But a rich one," Ramón observed.

"To some women that is no comfort," his sister informed him with a tart edge to her voice, "believe it or not."

Estela's husband, Esteban, spoke before Ramón could rise to this bit of provocation. "Let me point out, my dear, that we have no tickets and it is getting rather late. Besides, I don't believe Ramón's other guests are as enthusiastic as you about the program."

Señora Martínez made a deprecating gesture. "I am sorry if we cast a damper—is that correct?—on the outing. However, my husband and I have been several times to the ballet, and it is better this evening that we go home. We have a teenage daughter who is out with her young man, and we must be there to see that she returns at the appointed time. You understand?"

Estela protested, but the motherly woman would not be swayed. She insisted on leaving as soon as the coffee cups had been drained.

Her husband supported her. "No, truly," he said as they stood at the door. "Youth is the time of enjoyment. We would be most unhappy, Ramón, if we were to cause you to miss this opportunity of showing your beautiful fiancée the nightlife of our wonderful city on this her first visit."

Ramón, a thoughtful expression on his face, made no other attempt to keep them. Señor Martínez sketched a short bow in Anne's direction, then with a final American-style handshake, maneuvered himself and his wife out of the door.

"A fine idea," Doña Isabel said as they turned back into the room. "Even if the ballet is out of the question, there are other places to go in the evening."

"There is an excellent singer at one of the big hotels on the Paseo de la Reforma, and they have a good dance band," Estela added hopefully.

"You are taking up night life, Abuelita?" Estela's husband asked.

"Not at all. I value my rest too much to join you. I will naturally not go, but I am not so old that I have forgotten what it is like to be young with the night before me."

Esteban slanted a look at Ramón, his shoulders heaving in a resigned sigh. "We seem to be outnumbered."

"Except that we have not heard from Anne," Ramón agreed. "What do you say, *querida*? Do you wish to go?"

She did, very much. It seemed such an anticlimax to have the evening end after so short a time. There should be something more to do justice to the fineness of the dress she was wearing and the haunting sense of anticipation she felt. Still she hesitated, by no means certain that Ramón really wanted to know her wishes. It was possible, since hers would be the deciding vote, that he was waiting for her to decline.

She lifted her gaze to his, a small, perplexed frown between her eyes. As if sensing her dilemma, he moved to her side and, taking her hand, carried it to his lips. "It shall be as you say, my dove," he said.

The grip of his fingers was firm and reassuring, the tone of his voice caressing. In his eyes was an expression she had not seen before, a soft gleam that, regardless of her understanding of the role he was playing, brought a hint of color to her cheeks. She must be careful, she told herself, then forgot the warning a moment later as her fingers curled around those of the man beside her of their own accord.

"I would like to go, if you would," she replied, her mouth curving into a smile.

The lounge was plush, with velvet-covered seats in circular booths about small tables. The dim light of candles in red globes on each table was the only illumination. The band, in sequined jackets that winked in the semidarkness, was spotlighted on a raised dais with a small dance floor of smoked copper tiles surrounded by gold and red and black carpet directly in front of them. As Estela had promised, they were good, shifting effortlessly from one piece of music to the next, blending a half-dozen different types of music, from modern rock to Latin. The amplified sound was a little loud, but as the deferential waiter, with a greeting for

Ramón, led them to a table near the wall some distance away, that did not trouble them.

Drinks were ordered and they sat for a time over them in desultory conversation, with Estela pointing out various people, government officials, artists, and a number of acquaintances, to Anne. Several people stopped by their table and were introduced, though after a time Anne gave up even trying to remember their names. There were too many, the names were too unfamiliar, and it seemed unlikely she would ever meet them again.

When a slow dreamy song began, Ramón turned to Anne. "Well, *querida?*" he said, holding out his hand.

Anne got to her feet reluctantly. It had been ages since she had danced, not since she had left the children's home. The kind of men she had met had not been able to afford much more than a movie and a hamburger, in the way of a date. At the home there had been lessons given by the older boys and girls to the younger ones and the occasional Saturday-night dance party, nothing to give her confidence to move onto the floor with a man like Don Ramón Castillo. Still, she could hardly object without revealing to the others that they had never danced together.

"It's been a long time since I've tried to dance," she warned him as his arms closed around her.

"Don't worry about it," he said, his mouth against the silkiness of her hair. "Just relax and leave it to me."

It was good advice, but hard to accept. She was too aware of the touch of his fingers on her back through the thin silk of her dress, of the brush of his thighs against hers, and the tantalizingly masculine smell of the aftershave he had used. It was strangely comforting to be held close, to feel the strength of his shoulder beneath her hand, and yet she longed for the music to come to an end. Under the circumstances, dancing was not a pleasure but a refined torment.

Ramón bent his head and for a moment Anne thought he intended to press a kiss into the curve of her neck. Instead, he whispered, "You might at least try to look as if you are enjoying it."

Startled, she missed a step. "I'm sorry," she said automatically.

"Don't be," he said, drawing back to look down at her. "I'm not going to eat you. But if you don't smile, I'm going to kiss you right here."

At the unlikelihood of his carrying out the threat, the smile he had requested appeared. "You wouldn't," she said with conviction.

A glint of amusement in his eyes, he answered, "So you think, but you're taking no chances, are you? Ah, that's it. A look of positive affection. Hold it, please, because we are being watched by my darling cousin, Irene."

He covered her instant start of confusion with an expert gliding step. Her smile slipped, but she did not quite lose it. "I suppose we should not have come," she said, voicing the first thought that came into her head in order to regain her equilibrium.

"It doesn't matter, we had to meet her sometime," he reassured her. "I would have preferred to wait until later, but perhaps it's best this way. Don't be surprised if she and her escort manage to run into us as we leave the floor."

The music was slowing. As it stopped and they began to make their way with the other couples back to their table, Ramón kept her hand firmly clasped in his. They had not gone more than a few steps before Irene, with her escort in tow, barred their way.

"Cousin Ramón," she drawled, "and his little—"

"Good evening, cousin," Ramón said, overriding her

strident tones without apparent effort. "I didn't expect to see you here."

"No, I imagine not," Irene agreed, her gaze moving with studied insolence over Anne. Abruptly her eyes fastened on the pendant lying warm and glowing just above the soft curves of her breasts. The blood draining from her face, she gasped, "That necklace, she's wearing Tía Isabel's turquoise."

Anyone listening would have thought she had stolen it, Anne thought in rising irritation at being passed over as if she were incapable of hearing or speaking.

"A gift," Ramón answered stiffly.

"But it was to be mine, Irene said. "Tía Isabel always said she was saving it for—"

"For the woman I was to marry," he finished for her.

Irene took a deep, trembling breath. The action swelled the bodice of her tightly fitting dress of some heavy green material with a metallic sheen in its folds, and caused the long earrings of green and yellow feathers she was wearing to flutter against her neck. Suddenly Anne was reminded of a picture she had seen just that morning representing Quetzalcoatl, the Feathered Serpent of the Aztecs. At the ridiculousness of the idea, she was released from the paralizing self-consciousness that had held her stiff at Ramón's side. Now, turning to him, she placed her left hand with its sparkling diamond ring on the dark sleeve of his arm.

"Ramón, darling," she said softly, "I don't believe I have been officially introduced to your cousin."

"Forgive me," he said, covering her fingers with his own at once. "Anne, allow me to present to you my cousin Irene. Irene, my fiancée, Anne Matthews."

"How do you do," Anne said, holding out her free hand to the other woman with a smile that was perfectly cool and friendly. "I hope you will think of me as a cousin also, since we are all to be of the same family."

Shock turned the woman's face to wax. The fingers she placed in Anne's hand were nerveless and cold. Glancing at her in concern, her escort introduced himself with a few phrases, then began to make their excuses. Irene allowed herself to be led away, but the look she cast over her shoulder at Anne held the glitter of sheer malevolence made all the more potent for being mute.

As they returned to the table Estela scanned their faces, an anxious look in her eyes. When Anne was seated, she leaned forward. "I saw you stop to speak to Irene just now. I hope she was not—that she did not say anything unpleasant?"

"Not really," Anne answered, smiling again with lips that now felt stiff with the effort she had made to appear at ease.

Ramón, throwing a glance at Anne that was approving and yet faintly enigmatic, said, "I believe you could say that we held our own."

"I am sorry that you had to meet this soon, for I would not like you to judge all of Ramón's family by this cousin," Estela said earnestly.

Touched by the other girl's concern, Anne could only shake her head. It was Ramón who answered for her.

"How could she judge only by Irene when she has also met Abuelita—and you?" he asked, the lift of an eyebrow taking the sting from that barbed compliment.

In the general laughter the tension eased. Esteban ordered another round of drinks, though Anne refused hers. A small throb of pain had begun again in her temple. It grew more noticeable as she listened to the amplified voice of the singer Estela had recommended. He was Latin, with a caressing and hypnotic timbre in his voice, but she was glad when he was done. Not long afterward Ramón, watching her rubbing her temple through narrowed eyes, suggested that they leave.

Estaban and Estela did not come into the house when they reached home. After an exchange of good nights they got into their low sports car sitting on the drive and drove away. Ramón left his car for the chauffeur to put away and followed Anne into the house.

Inside the entrance hall he touched her arm, turning her to face him. "It's your head, isn't it?"

She nodded, then winced. The pain had grown gradually worse on the drive home and even that small movement set off an alarming reaction.

"I should not have let you go," he said, frowning. "I would not have, except you looked so much like an orphan child on Christmas morning after your one gift is opened, wondering if that is to be all."

At the sudden stricken look in her eyes, he cursed under his breath and stepped closer to take her in his arms. "That was stupid. Forgive me, Anne. For a moment I forgot—"

His sympathy combined with the nerve-racking events of the past few days was almost too much. As she felt the hurtful rise of tears against her throat, she broke free of the arm holding her.

"That's all right," she said on a quick indrawn breath without looking at him. "You don't have to apologize. I—I enjoyed the evening."

Blindly she turned toward the stairs. Her foot was on the bottom step when he called after her.

"You have something for your headache?"

"Yes, the doctor left a few capsules," she managed, and then because her voice was treacherously near to breaking, she fled.

In her room, she took off the turquoise and laid it carefully on the dressing table, removed her dress and hung it away, then slipped into her gown. She removed the light makeup she had applied, brushed her hair, and swallowed one of the capsules left on the table beside her bed before sliding between the covers. Only then did she allow the threatening tears to trickle from her eyes. They slid hot and salty into her hairline. But before the first had dried, she was asleep.

On Ramón's orders, breakfast was brought to her in bed. The tray was set with a delicate china patterned with small pink roses which she had not seen before, and adorned with a single pink rosebud in a crystal vase. Two notes lay folded on a tiny silver salver. The first, from Ramón, contained only the suggestion that she spend the morning in bed and the offer of books and magazines from his study to entertain her. The second in the spidery handwriting of Doña Isabel held out the inducement of luncheon in town and an afternoon of shopping. Listless from a night of overheavy slumber, it seemed too much trouble to do anything other than fall in with their wishes. She had the nagging feeling that she should be doing something constructive to earn her salary, but as she had no idea what the duties of a fiancée consisted of, she could not bring herself to move.

Thinking of the salary reminded her that Ramón had not mentioned the amount she was to be paid for this unusual employment. She must remember to tell him to deduct the amount of the clothing he had supplied from the total, though she had the melancholy suspicion that if she was to be paid an amount equal to two week's salary at Metcalf's there would be nothing left when the price of the dresses was subtracted. No matter. She could not and would not accept them from him, especially after last night. An orphan she might be; still, she had no need of his charity.

Her suspicions were amply proved that afternoon. As she followed Doña Isabel in and out of the smart shops of the "pink zone," the most cosmopolitan area in the city bounded by Avenida Insurgentes, Avenida Chapultepec, Florencia Street, and the Paseo de la Reforma, she grew more and more certain that she had been wrong to accept so much from Ramón. Even after she had mentally translated pesos into dollars, nothing was cheap. Further along some of the streets she saw the signs of smaller, less-expensive-looking boutiques that looked as if she might have been able to afford their wares, but Doña Isabel had no interest in such places. She unerringly chose the most exclusive establishments and marched in, her bearing so regal that she commanded instant service. In one or two of the shops she was recognized by the more mature salesladies and greeted like a long-lost friend. Each time this happened, she introduced Anne as her future granddaughter-in-law, with the subtle insinuation that it would be well to treat her with the deference due a prospective customer. If the proper show of interest was forthcoming, the old lady allowed herself to be persuaded to recount the story, slightly altered to fit the circumstances, of how her grandson, an impetuous lover unable to face the thought of leaving his new fiancée behind in Dallas, had practically kidnapped her. According to Doña Isabel, he had swept her off her feet and carried her on board his plane in the most romantic abduction ever dreamed of by woman. Being a man, he had counted as unimportant the fact that Anne had no clothing or personal effects, not even a lipstick. When Anne tried to protest that Ramón had seen to her more pressing needs, it only appreared that she was trying to defend him, at which the older women had exchanged knowing smiles. After that it did no good for her to insist she needed nothing. Doña Isabel, ignoring her objections, ordered sets of casual clothes in delicious shades of green and pink and sherbet orange. It had to be admitted, however, that these appeared as insignificant as Doña Isabel pretended beside the dozens of suits, dresses, and evening gowns she pointed out to be delivered to the house for herself.

They did not wait to be fitted. Doña Isabel declared they did not have the time. They would make their decisions at home in privacy and simply return what they did not like. Anne said nothing, finding it more than useless. But she vowed she would return everything the old lady had bought her later. Somehow she would make her understand how she felt. She would not be indebted to either her or her grandson for another penny. It left her in much too vulnerable a position for her peace of mind.

After a little more than three hours Anne thought Doña Isabel began to flag. Her spirits and enthusiasm remained high and her back was as straight as when she had set out, but she looked a little pale, a little blue around the mouth, under her dusting of face powder, and she had begun to look around unconsciously for a chair each time they entered a new shop. She was no longer young, after all, and was unaccustomed to so much activity. It would not have been very tactful to say so, however.

"Doña Isabel, is there a coffee shop somewhere near?" Anne asked as they emerged from the cool dimness of yet another shop in the fading light of late afternoon.

"I'm not certain, but I feel sure there is. You feel the need of refreshment, my dear?"

"Yes, please. I hate to be a nuisance. I'm afraid that ridiculous bump on the head took more out of me than I can realize."

"Why didn't you say something sooner? I'm a thoughtless old woman. We will go home at once," Doña Isabel said, turning toward where the chauffeur waited beside the long black limousine not far away.

"I'm sorry that you had to cut short your shopping

because of me," Anne said when they were seated and the long car had glided out into the breakneck flow of traffic at that time of day.

"Not at all. In truth, I was beginning to be a little tired myself. Does your head ache?"

"A bit," Anne replied. It was no more than the truth. The slanting rays of the sun reflecting from the gleaming chrome and the waxed finish of the car seemed to stab into her eyes.

A tiny frown between her eyes, the old lady surveyed her face. "We'll have you home presently. Just sit back and relax."

Anne gave her a faint smile before turning away. She felt such a fraud. To change the subject and indicate to Doña Isabel that she was still well enough to take an interest in her surroundings, she pointed toward a statue they were passing, one of many along this wide, modern street, forming an interesting contrast with the glass and steel skyscrapers that backed them.

"Is that an Indian?" she asked.

"Indeed yes. That is Cuauhtemoc, the last of the Aztec emperors. He stands as a monument to the Aztec heritage of Mexico. As a people we are proud of this part of our past. Many of the best families of the city have the blood of the Aztec Indians in their veins, including the Castillo family. You were aware of this, were you not?"

"I suspected it, yes," Anne admitted.

"Ramón's ancestors were traditionally warriors instead of farmers or artisans, knights of the ocelot—or the *tigre*, as they were named by the Spanish who tried to conquer them. It troubles you that Ramón has this blood?"

"Troubles me?" Anne turned to face her, puzzled.

"You do not feel it is a taint? For it is not so, I assure you. To be descended of the Aztecs is a thing of,

pride in Mexico, as much so as being linked to a race
of kings."

"No, of course I don't consider it a taint," Anne exclaimed. "Such a thing never crossed my mind."

Doña Isabel gave a satisfied nod. "It is good. You
will find such a heritage of great value to your children
and your children's children."

The implication of the old lady's words took Anne's
breath for an instant. "Doña Isabel," she said at last in
a low voice. "You know that will never be. You must
not—"

The old lady lifted her hand in a commanding gesture, indicating the chauffeur in front of them with a
tilt of her head. Anne fell silent, oppressed suddenly by
the falseness of her position. The chauffeur, so far as she
knew, understood little English. Why should she have
to pretend for his sake? And though she tried to tell
herself that Doña Isabel was right in being so cautious,
the words she had used, the vision she had conjured up
of beautiful dark-eyed, straight-limbed children with
Aztec blood in their veins would not be banished from
Anne's mind, nor would the odd hurt that thinking of
them caused.

Chapter 5

Doña Isabel did not come down for dinner. An hour before time, she sent word by Carmelita that she was more tired than she had realized and intended to have a tray in her room, adding the request that Anne keep Ramón company downstairs. Left to herself, Anne might have taken the coward's way and asked for a tray also, but Doña Isabel had neatly circumvented that. With a sigh, she asked Carmelita if she would be expected to dress for dinner.

A little later, wearing the gold sleeveless knit with the silk-fringed shawl, draped over her elbows in the accepted manner by the admiring little maid, Anne descended to the sala. She had rested briefly after returning from shopping and her headache had receded once more. Carmelita had brushed her hair into a shining bell and, using the cosmetics sent by Ramón, shadowed her eyes lightly with a turquoise powder brushed with gold. She felt confident, even attractive, more so than she had ever felt in her life. She felt, in fact, equal to whatever the occasion might demand.

Ramón, exotically handsome in a velvet jacket of dark gray worn with black trousers and a gold silk print shirt open at the neck in the continental fashion, turned at her entrance. A fire against the coolness of the evening air burned in the room. Anne could not be certain that the gleam of welcome and approval she

81

thought she saw in Ramón's eyes was not also a reflection of the fire's bright warmth.

"Don't tell me," he greeted Anne with wry humor, "let me guess. You had a note from Abuelita also?"

Anne had to admit it.

"You must forgive her. She means to be tactful. I'm sure, at any rate, that she would approve of my arrangements for dinner. I thought we would have it here beside the fire, unless you object?"

"Not at all," Anne said. "It should be nicer than at the long table in the dining room."

As she seated herself in the chair he held for her, María entered the room to announce that dinner was ready to be served. Swinging to Anne, Ramón asked, "You are ready now? Or would you like a glass of wine first?"

When Anne waved away the offer of an apéritif, he instructed María to begin, then waited until their first course was placed in front of them before he returned to the subject of his grandmother.

"Tell me, Anne," he said, his deep, slightly accented voice giving her name a strange sound in her ears, "what do you think of Abuelita's health? As an impartial observer, does she seem as strong to you as she pretends?"

Lifting the heavy silver soup spoon beside her plate, Anne answered slowly. "It's difficult to say. Until this afternoon I would have answered yes, easily, but now I'm not so sure."

When she had gone on to explain what she meant, Ramón shook his head. "She is seventy-three years old, a great age, and she will not admit to any infirmity unless it suits her purpose. That's the trouble. I can never be sure when she feels really ill and when she is shamming in order to have her way."

"You worry about her a great deal," Anne said, a statement rather than a question.

"Why not? Other than Estela, who is quite naturally involved with her husband and children, she is all I have."

That was not strictly true. There was Irene with her small head, slanted eyes, and reptilian grace. At the thought of her the hot soup, so aromatic and delicious a moment before, turned tasteless in Anne's mouth.

"The shopping expedition was successful?" Ramón asked.

"Oh, yes," she agreed, summoning her wits to describe, since his interest seemed real, some of the many dresses and evening gowns Doña Isabel had ordered. She did not mention the boxes that had been delivered with those of his grandmother and that now reposed on chairs in her own bedroom.

Slanting her an enigmatic glance, he said, "It begins to look as though Abuelita has not forgotten the party she spoke of last night, or the visits she will have to entertain from her friends afterward."

"I believe she plans to lead a more active life from now on," Anne agreed with care.

"That will be good, so long as she keeps it within reason. I appreciate what you did this afternoon, persuading her to return home. I hope I can depend on you to take as good care of her in the future?"

Anne looked up at him. "I will do my best, for as long as I am here," she said, meeting his intent gaze without flinching.

He did not look away. "I'm sure you will always do your best, which reminds me. I have not expressed my gratitude for the way you played the role of my fiancée last night. You were very convincing."

Memory of the night and its aftermath made her voice tight as she answered, "I tried to be."

"Estela was quite taken with you. She phoned me this morning to tell me we were perfect for each other.

I'm afraid she will be most disappointed when we part."

Anne searched his face with its sardonic calm for some hint of his feelings. She found none. "I'm sorry someone as nice as Estela has to be involved."

He had been playing idly with his wineglass; now his fingers tightened on it for an instant before he lifted it to his lips. "So am I," he replied.

When the meal was over and cleared away, they sat on before the replenished fire. Silence stretched between them, silence that was neither comfortable nor uncomfortable. Anne fumbled through her mind for something to say and found nothing. She could sense tension in the man lounging in the deep chair beside her, almost as if he placed some form of restraint upon himself in her presence. From where she sat his face was in the shadow, but she could see his right hand resting on the arm of his chair, his fingers curled around the tapestry-covered end. Suddenly her gaze riveted on the gold and black enameled signet ring that he wore as she realized the significance of it. Knights of the tigre, the Spanish had called them, Aztec warriors of the ocelot. In the bold, proud profile of the man seated beside her, it was almost as if one of that breed had come to life. Shivering a little, she looked away into the heart of the fire.

Disturbed by her movement, he turned his head. "You have plans for tomorrow?" he asked abruptly.

"Your grandmother didn't mention any."

"You have none of your own?" he insisted, a trace of impatience in his voice.

She shook her head. "I would like to see something of your country, but I don't want to be a bother, or to go off on my own when I might be needed."

A frown, as if he intended to say something sharp, appeared between his eyes, then faded. When he spoke, his tone was mild. "I would rather you did not go about alone. I have a few business matters to attend to in the morning, but in the afternoon we might drive out to see the pyramids at Teotihuacán."

Anne flicked a glance at him. What she had expected she did not know. His face revealed nothing more than calm courtesy. "Are you sure you won't be bored?"

"It is some time since I was there, when I was a college student, in fact. People always ignore the attractions on their own doorstep, don't they? Besides, Estela will expect to hear that you have been sightseeing, becoming more knowledgeable about Mexico than the Mexicans. We wouldn't want to disappoint her."

Stung by such a dutiful attitude, Anne said, "You don't have to come. I'm sure there is a bus or some other means of transportation I could use."

"True," he replied, his tone tinged with a satirical humor, "but I'm afraid you will have to put up with my company. I am unwilling to have you venturing about the streets of Mexico without protection from the unpleasantness, if not actual danger, that can befall a woman without an attentive escort. No, please," he went on as she opened her mouth to argue, "I can do no less. Estela and Abuelita will expect it."

Stiffly, Anne agreed and a time was set immediately after luncheon.

"There will be much walking, and also, it is possible to climb the largest structure, the Pyramid of the Sun. Comfortable shoes are necessary and some form of slacks or a suit with pants."

"All right," she answered.

"There is a restaurant at the site where we can have dinner. If you would like to try it, I will make reservations."

"I would like that very much," Anne murmured, touched by this example of his thoughtfulness, which

seemed to indicate that his offer had not been made on
the spur of the moment. She wished she had been
more gracious in her acceptance, but the moment was
gone. With a satisfied nod, he turned away, back to his
contemplation of the fire.

Not long afterward, Anne, pressed by the growing
conviction that Ramón would prefer to be alone, said
good night. With the perfect manners she had come
to expect from him, he got to his feet to see her to the
stairs. Halfway up, she turned to see him standing in
the double opening of the sala, with the light from the
stained-glass fixture falling on his face. The lozenges of
red and amber and black gave him the look of a pen-
sive Satan left alone in Hades. The feeling crept in
upon her that she was wrong to go, that if she had
stayed there might have been a demand made of her fit
to test her newfound confidence. It was not a feeling
to encourage sleep.

The morning brought a special-delivery air-mail let-
ter from Iva containing her salary check as promised,
plus two pages filled with anxious questions and warnings. There was no sign of the suitcase she expected
from Judy, and Carmelita, on being questioned, denied
all knowledge of any such arrival, though she promised
to speak to the other servants, especially the chauffeur,
who would have had to pick it up at the airport. The
results of the inquiry were exactly nil. No one had seen
such a thing, nor had there been any calls from the airport concerning anything of that nature. It seemed
petty to carry such a problem to Ramón; he had so
many things so much more important to occupy his
mind. But she did not know what else to do. She did
not, however, have the opportunity to put it to him.
By the time she descended to the patio he had break-
fasted and gone.

As she ate her own breakfast of hot rolls, fresh butter, coffee, strawberries, and papaya, she vowed that if

her suitcase did not turn up by the next day she would call Judy. It was always possible that Iva had failed to impress on her roommate the importance of packing Anne's things and shipping them off without delay.

In the meantime she had little choice but to don one of the pantsuits Doña Isabel had chosen for her. The short skirt of her cream-colored suit, coming just above the knee was not exactly the thing for climbing pyramids, and in any case, she was heartily sick of it. With a kind of wry self-knowledge, she realized she was not sorry to have an excuse for wearing some of the beautiful things that had been bought for her on their shopping trip. If she was not careful, she would be thoroughly spoiled by the time she left Mexico, with little chance for happiness anywhere else. It would be easy to become used to the beauty and wealth that surrounded her, far too easy. She could have refused to go until her own clothing had arrived, of course, but she had a fair idea of what Ramón's reaction to that excuse would be; he had so little patience with her compunction about taking anything from him. In addition, she did not like to alter the arrangements he had made to take her sightseeing. He was under no compulsion to do so, and there was also the risk he would decide not to take her at all.

Anne appeared for luncheon in a two-piece suit of azalea-pink cotton polyester with a linen weave. With it went a blouse in a soft aqua and pink print and a small scarf of the same material that she tied around her hair to hold it back out of her face. A touch of pink lip gloss and a brush of aqua shadow over her eyes completed her makeup. She looked fresh and feminine, and at the same time practical with her tied-back hair and sensible shoes of camel leather with crepe soles and low wedge heels.

Ramón did not appear for luncheon. It was a delicious though solitary meal. Served on the patio, it consisted of seafood soup, tacos, guacamole salad, and an odd fruit with a smooth custard taste that the shy, Indian maidservant called a chirimoya.

She lingered over the meal as long as possible, but when at last the maidservant began to hover as though she would like to clear away, and possibly take the time for her afternoon rest, Anne finally crumpled her napkin and dropped it beside her plate. Leaving the table, she passed through the arched opening with its wrought-iron gate that led from the patio to the garden. A stone walk bordered by ferns led around the side of the house, paralleling the whitewashed wall that protected the house from the street. At the foot of the wall were planted clove pinks, their spicy fragrance filling the air, vying with the sweet scent of the roses and sweet peas growing in a tangled mass upon the wall. Carnations grown lanky sprawled over the wall, laying their bright, fluffy heads of red and yellow and pink in her path. Above her head arched a sky as blue as the turquoise Doña Isabel had given her while through the trees she could glimpse the serrated purple teeth of the distant mountains.

Drunk on fragrance, she stopped under an overhanging bower of roses, lifting her face to the gentle touch of the sun, letting a vagrant breeze stir soft tendrils of hair about her face. The moments passed. A bee buzzed gently about her head, a quartet of yellow butterflies danced past her at no more than arm's length, and a small green lizard darted out to lie panting inches from her shoe upon the stone walk. Caught in a moment of infinite enjoyment, she dared not move for fear of shattering something precious.

Abruptly the lizard scuttled away. Turning her head slightly, she saw Ramón, framed in the arched entrance to the patio. As their eyes met, he pushed away from the wall and came toward her. Reaching above her head, he pulled one of the small blush pink roses from the vine and stood for a moment, twirling it between his fingers, a small, almost derisive smile quirking the corner of his mouth. Then with a quick movement, he thrust it just above her ear, pushing the stem under the scarf that held back her hair. With a finger beneath her chin, he tilted her lips to meet his. Anne felt a quick, gentle pressure, and then he raised his head. Trapped in the unexpected poignance of the moment, she could not move, could not speak.

And then, his voice shockingly prosaic, Ramón asked, "You have eaten?"

Anne managed to nod.

Dropping his hand, he caught her fingers. "So have I. Let us go before it is too late," he said, his grip tightening on her hand.

Teotihuacán, twenty-six miles northeast of Mexico City, was reached by an express toll road. Beyond the edge of the city the route they covered was flat, arid, and open, bounded only by the ring of amethyst-blue mountains. To the east lay the dry bed of Lake Texcoco, and beyond it, obscured by heat haze and the rising forms of dust devils and cloud vapor, were the snow-capped volcanic peaks of Iztaccihuatl and Popocatepetl. Small yellow wildflowers made their homes in the ditches beside the road, competing for moisture with a half-dozen or more different kinds of cacti. Organ cactus, thorny sentinels, stood here and there, their blossoms perched among their spikes like exotic birds resting in flight. Prickly pear sprawled in patches, and once they passed an agave, the famed century plant, in blossom with its small greenish-white umbels towering thirty feet and more above the gray-green swordlike leaves of the plant.

Seeing her interest, Ramón told her what this plant, known locally as the maguey, had meant in times past to the Indians and Mexican peasants. It had once been a rarity to see one in bloom. Just before time for it to flower, the heart had been cut from it and the side leaves used to cover over the cavity. The juice that would have gone to the great stem of the flower then filled this basin. The honey-sweet juice thus produced, numbering from one hundred and twenty-five to two hundred gallons, was then drawn off and fermented to form a slightly alcoholic beverage called pulque, one of the most wholesome and refreshing drinks in the world, though somewhat strong in odor. This juice, at a certain period in its fermentation, was said to be good for the cleaning and healing of wounds. Distilled, it forms an alcoholic drink that was one of the mainstays of the Mexican economy, tequila. There were many uses for the leaves and stems. Dried, the older side leaves were good for thatching roofs. The new growth, when the spines were removed and the fleshy stems chopped, were used as cattle feed. From the fibers of the leaves could be taken a strong thread called pita, from which could be made a tough brown paper, or when twisted together, a strong material that could be taken to make cloth, heavy-duty mesh bags, even rope. Even the roots of the plants could be used as a starchy food not unlike potatoes. Many of the cacti, so dangerous and untouchable to the eyes of norteamericanos, served a useful purpose. The organ cactus when planted close together made a strong and impenetrable fence for penning cattle. Birds hollowed out holes for their nests in them, causing injuries that were fed upon by larva, which in turn fed the birds. Nature wasted nothing, nor, as Ramón pointed out, had the Indian. It was not, in these days of environmental concern, a new observation, and yet, to find the same attitude among the Mexican Indians as was so often portrayed among the American tribes was oddly comforting, though Anne could not have explained why.

It had not been an easy drive. When he was not pointing out some feature of the landscape to her attention, Ramón was withdrawn, busy with his own thoughts. He had dispensed with the limousine and chaffeur, driving himself in a low-slung coffee-colored sports car. He sent the car hurtling along the road with swift precision, his well-formed hands steady upon the wheel. When the subject of the cacti was exhausted, Anne, uncertain of his mood, fell silent.

At last they saw the pyramids from a distance, Great weathered stone cones rising from the plain. The site of the ruins covered several square miles, including a parking lot dotted with cars and the large chartered buses of tourists.

Leaving the car, they visited the museum at the entrance. Inside, Anne stared in solemn concentration at the shattered fragments of knives and arrows made of obsidian, shards of pottery, and other exhibits that indicated that Teotihuacán had been a thriving center covering several hundred acres, with lime-plaster-paved streets and a complete system of underground drainage. She was fascinated also by the tiny idols with blank eyes made of clay, which had been found lying all about, and the stone representations of the huge figures of the gods of the sun and the moon, which, covered with gold, had stood at the site until destroyed by the early Spanish priests.

The builders of Teotihuacán, she found, were not Aztecs but a much earlier people who were thought to have been traders with dominion over a large expanse of the country. Their culture had reached its zenith sometime between three hundred to four hundred A.D. Archaeologists agreed that for some unknown reason, perhaps in flight from the warlike Toltec Indians, they had deserted their city after destroying it themselves and attempting to burn it.

As the evening progressed, the tourist buses began to roll back toward Mexico City. When the crowd had thinned to a few scattered groups with the look of

students or working archaeologists about them, Anne
and Ramón walked down the straight street lined with
the ruins of ancient platforms known as the Avenue of
the Dead, which led to the Pyramid of the Moon. This
cone was slightly smaller than the Pyramid of the Sun,
which sat to its left, but it had been built on an eleva-
tion so that the two structures were of the same
height. Anne had known the pyramids were huge, but
she had not realized how really enormous they were
until she stood with her head back, staring up at the
ascending steps. High above, where an ancient temple
had stood on the Pyramid of the Sun, could be seen
the antlike figures of a few who had climbed the steep
steps up the face of its five terraces earlier.

Those steps, without stair rails, were every bit as steep
as they looked. As she climbed, she could use the steps
above her for a handhold, and with Ramón following
close beneath her, she was doubly glad that she had decided to take his advice and wear the pink pantsuit. It
did not help her feelings to have to lean to one side to
allow the student party in their cut-off jeans to clamber
unconcernedly past her on their way down, leaving the
silent platform at the top to Ramón and herself.

The climb, all two hundred ten feet of it, was worth
every alarm it caused. The view from the top was
breathtaking. Teotihuacán lay stretched out around
them, much clearer in its ancient outline than from
ground level. Beyond it spread the brown and green
plains shimmering in the pure, limpid light with the
sun dropping low in the brilliant azure sky, banded like
a skirt by the encircling purple mountains.

Standing with his shoulders back and his hands
resting on his hips, staring out over the platform of
gray-old stone, Ramón broke the silence. "They once
thought these mounds were used for burial, like the pyramids of Egypt, until they excavated and discovered
their mistake. They know now they were used for reli-

gious purposes, one of mankind's more obvious attempts to come nearer to the thing he worships. But I've always wondered if the height and stature of these pyramids, which lift whoever climbs them high into the clouds, were not an illustration of the meaning of the name Teotihuacán."

"Meaning?" Anne asked softly, half-afraid the sound of her voice would break into the mood that gripped him.

"Teotihuacán," he quoted. "The place 'where men became gods.'"

Slowly he turned to Anne, a look in his eyes that was half-mockery at his own fancy, half an invitation for her to join him in it. The slanting rays of the sun struck across his cheekbones, gilding the planes of his face. Deep within she felt a strange, burgeoning pain. Her throat closed, swelling as if against the onrush of sudden tears. Taking a deep breath, she turned, moving away a few steps to stare out blindly over the flat terrain. It was silly of her to be so moved. Why should an expression on his face in the sunset affect her in such a way? The effects of the knock on the head, no doubt. It must be that, combined with some atmosphere that lingered here in this ancient place. That was what it was, nothing more.

The scrape of a footstep behind her caused a sensation like the approach of danger to ripple over her skin. She did not turn, though she knew he was beside her.

"What is it? Are you all right?" he asked.

"Of course I'm all right," she said, trying to smile though she did not quite meet his eyes.

"Some people find out they are affected by heights only after they reach the top of the ladder," he explained his concern. "You don't have to be brave about it."

"I'm not being brave," she replied, her voice more positive as she hit on a way to distract his attention from herself. "Tell me how these pyramids were used in the Indian religion." After a moment he complied.

"Little is known about the Teotihuacán, but if, as is suspected, they set the pattern for the Aztecs who came several hundred years later, they worshiped the powers of nature, the sun and the moon, the wind and the rain. Without these things they could not live, and so it was necessary for the spirits of these gods to remain strong. They had to be nourished, and what better nourishment than the spirits of men that were enclosed in their hearts?"

"You mean—human sacrifice,"

"Yes. The sacrifice of the hearts of enemy warriors torn living from their open breasts. The hearts of the bravest of the enemy warriors were the hardest to acquire, and because of it, were more valuable. War could not be won without sacrifice, sacrifice was not possible without captive warriors, captives were not available without military victory. It was an unending cycle."

"A terrible one," Anne commented tightly.

"Was it? In a time when so-called civilized nations sacked towns and put the entire population to the sword? When men and women in Europe were being tortured and burned for no more than the religious beliefs of those in power? In Indochina in the last few years hundreds of thousands have been killed solely because of their political views. Human beings have never been noted for their kindness to their enemies."

When she still looked doubtful, he went on in a reflective tone. "I'm not condoning human sacrifice, only pointing out that barbarity depends on your viewpoint. For instance, the Aztecs never struck a child in punishment until he was of an age to understand what he had done wrong, at eight years old. And criminals were not imprisoned; they were enslaved to the person they had injured most so they could repair the damage done as well as expiate their crimes."

"Both of those make sense," Anne was forced to admit.

"I suppose what I'm trying to say is," Ramón said slowly, "don't judge another culture, another people, too quickly. Get to know them before you make up your mind."

Was there a hidden meaning in his words? Anne would have liked to think so, but was afraid it was only in her own mind.

They remained on the pyramid for some time, talking idly. With a question or two Anne drew more of the details of the life style of the Aztecs from Ramón and from there he was launched into the history of their conquest by Cortes.

Tiring of standing, they took a seat on the top step of the great staircase and Anne sat with elbows on her knees, listening in fascination. It was true, as Doña Isabel had said. Ramón was proud of his Indian heritage. But he was just as mindful of his Spanish blood also and gave equal credit to the bravery and daring of the men who had voyaged so far to pillage another civilization. She heard for the first time of Doña Marina, the Aztec maiden who had betrayed her people for the sake of her love for Cortes, and sitting there in the growing purple dusk, on the site of an Indian temple, it seemed as if it could have happened only yesterday instead of five hundred years ago.

At last Ramón got to his feet and held out his hand. "We had better go before it gets too dark to get down without breaking our necks."

Anne agreed with reluctance. It had been so companionable sitting there. With the return to responsibility Ramón's attitude had changed, become casual and at the same time distant. The feel of his fingers drawing her to her feet was electric, but something in his manner made her move carefully, resisting the impulse to lean on his strength. She was just as careful going down the steep stone stairway. She felt instinctively that if he should stumble she would be in danger of more than a broken neck.

When they reached the bottom, Ramón broke the increasingly tense silence. "Tired?" he asked.

"A little."

"A reservation was made for us at the restaurant here as planned, but we need not keep it if you would rather return to town."

The reservation was a concession, she realized. The evening was still much too early for Ramón to be thinking of dinner. Used to the late hours kept in his country, his appetite would not begin to awaken for another two hours or more. Anne, though she was growing used to late breakfast and luncheon, could not seem to control a wistful longing for her supper when evening came. She had not realized that Ramón knew, however.

"Are you certain you want to eat so early?" she asked, aware in the back of her mind of an inclination to prolong the day.

"It shall be as you like," he said, a smile softening the formality of the reply.

"Then I would like it, very much," she answered.

Grilled beef was their main dish, served with potatoes that had been browned, then steamed with peppers and onion. Tasting it carefully, Anne decided the meat had also been rubbed with pepper before grilling.

"We will send it back to the kitchen if it is not to your liking and order something else," Ramón said, noticing her look of concentration. The explanation of what she was doing started a conversation on food that led to her job with Metcalf's. Before she realized it, Anne found herself telling him about her relationship with Joe and Iva, her position in the business, some of the perils and pleasures of catering, and one or two of the more humorous incidents that had occurred.

"You enjoyed your job?" he asked, an odd inflection in his voice.

"Yes—yes, I did," Anne said, her smile fading. "That is, I do." Her chin came up as she realized that she had been in danger of forgetting Ramón's suspicion of her. No doubt he had expected to find that she hated working at Metcalf's, that she was desperate to get away. He would be disappointed, no doubt, to find it wasn't so. Though she hated to acknowledge it even to herself, there was something else she had come close to forgetting. That was the fact that she would be returning to Metcalf's when this Mexican episode was over.

Not long afterward, Ramón signaled for their check and they left the restaurant.

The drive home was uneventful. Once or twice Ramón spoke, but she made such short answers that he did not persist. She thought he glanced at her in the dim light of the dashboard instruments, but she kept her eyes straight ahead, staring at the highway unwinding before them.

Ramón swung the sports car through the gates in the whitewashed wall, and with precision drew up before the front door and switched off the motor. In the sudden quiet Anne felt an awkward unease. Trying to ignore it, she turned in the seat.

"Thank you for taking me to Teotihuacán. I enjoyed it very much," she said primly.

Her right hand was on the door handle when he reached across to catch her wrist, holding her in place with his forearm.

"That was a nice little speech," he said, "like a school girl taken to see relatives."

"You forgot to say an orphan schoolgirl."

He was quiet a moment. "I thought that was forgotten. What made you think of it again? We were doing so well—or at least I thought so."

"Yes, weren't we? You were conducting a catechism, trying to find some clue to my terrible crime of forcing myself on you, instead of believing the simple truth: that it was an accident!"

"Is that the way it seemed?" he asked, his dark gaze piercing.

Defiantly she answered. "Yes, it is!"

"But isn't that an improvement," he suggested, "that I look for reasons other than greed and the grasping at a rich man?"

"Not to me it isn't," she returned, then slanted him an uncertain look from under her lashes.

"I acquit you of wanting my money, and you say it isn't important."

"You still think I'm a liar," she said, compressing her lips.

He shifted, releasing her wrist, placing his arm across the seat behind her back as she made no move to leave the car.

"But such an enchanting one," he told her, a soft, caressing note in his voice.

She swung her head, incensed at his agreement, ready to blast him for it. The words were smothered on her lips as he slipped his arm behind her and drew her close against him. His mouth burned on hers, setting the blood to racing in her veins. The fingers of his left hand touched her cheek, then trailed down the tender curve of her neck to the pearl buttons that closed the neckline of her blouse.

Anne wanted to remain aloof, but as his kiss deepened and his firm, sure touch brought its response, her hands, pressed in restraint against his chest, lost their strength. She felt herself drawn closer and closer until her body seemed almost to merge with his and still she was not close enough. His lips explored the moist corner of her mouth and slid with sensuous fire over the smooth angle of her jawline.

"Ramón," she breathed in a husky protest as his head dropped lower, brushing a warm kiss across the soft curves of her breasts where the vee neck of her blouse parted.

He went still. The soft whisper of their breathing was the only sound in the strained silence within the car.

With an effort that was as plain as it was controlled, he raised his head, drawing away. His hands went to her arms, moving down them to her wrists, which he crossed one over the other and placed in her lap. Anne could not see his face clearly, but she thought his rigid self-control was overlaid with the hauteur of Spanish pride. He did not speak. Opening the door on his side, he got out and walked around to open her door, holding it, making no effort to help her as she got out of the low-slung vehicle.

As they walked together up the stone walk to the entrance, Anne found herself wishing she had remained silent. His withdrawal after their closeness left her feeling bereft and with a cold feeling inside that had nothing to do with the mountain coolness of the night.

Their footsteps slowed as they reached the door and for a moment Anne thought he hesitated, on the verge of speaking, then the heavy, carved panel swung open.

The housekeeper moved back as they stepped over the threshold. Closing the door behind them, she said a soft "*Buenas noches*" and moved away with her stately tread down the hall.

Watching Mariá out of sight, Ramón sighed, then turned to Anne.

"For you, it has been a long day," he said, picking up her hand and carrying it to lips, whose ardor had grown cool, "Too long, perhaps. It is time for you also to say goodnight."

She did not like the hint that she was still an invalid, still less did she enjoy the implication that she was overwrought. On the other hand, she was not sure enough of her ground to argue with him about it.

"Yes," she said, her voice a husky whisper and her eyes bright with tears of anger. "Goodnight."

She resisted the impulse to look back as she went up the stairs. Inside her room she let her shoulders sag as she moved across to stand staring out the window. She was a fool; she must be to stay in Mexico knowing what Ramón Castillo thought of her. To let herself be swayed by an old woman, to take clothes and even jewelry from her and her grandson, what were these if not the acts of a fool? And now to allow Ramón to make love to her—what could be worse?

There was something worse, something more foolhardy.

Driving away from Teotihuacán she had looked back at those barbaric stone monuments shining in the moonlight and she had known then and was doubly certain now: it was not only the ancient Aztec warriors who had given up their hearts on the moon-silvered heights of the Pyramid of the Sun.

Chapter 6

Doña Isabel had not forgotten the engagement party. On the morning following Anne's visit to Teotihuacán she sent for Anne to discuss the affair. When the old lady began to sigh over the hundred and one details that must be seen to by way of preparation, Anne offered her help. As a result, she spent the next three days in close collaboration with Doña Isabel and María. Her principal function was to make endless lists. It took the best part of one day to decide who was to be invited, including the discussion of many contemporaries of the old lady who were no longer living and the chuckles the two older women indulged in over Anne's attempts to spell the unfamiliar names. Another morning was devoted to the type and amount of food and drink that would be served. Anne was able to be of help in this area, which speeded the process of decision-making considerably, especially when it came to settling the brisk argument between Doña Isabel and her longtime housekeeper over the rival merits of pink and plain champagne. Then there was the question of the floral decorations. Doña Isabel wanted to use flowers from their own gardens, a practice María, mindful of the family honor, did not hesitate to call shabby and too much like making do. A pointed reminder of the number of gardeners employed in the household did not move the housekeeper, nor did the claim that if they used the services of a florist their entertainment would look like that of everyone else. María would have no part of it. Open warfare was prevented only by Anne's rather diffident suggestion that flowers symbolic of the two countries of the principals be used. It was agreed, and an order placed for massed arrangements of American Beauty roses and bright yellow dahlias softened with greenery and white gypsophila. Anne made no objection to the last addition, but neither did she mention that in the United States the dainty white flower called gypsophila were known as baby's breath.

All the worry, the decisions, and the lists were unnecessary. The entire affair could have been turned over to Ramón's staff. Doña Isabel would have had no more to do then choose the gown she would wear and enjoy herself. She had repudiated the suggestion with scorn. Such a thing was well enough when Ramón was entertaining business associates; it would not do for her grandson's engagement. Doña Isabel assured Anne that Ramón was content so long as he knew his grandmother was not trying to shoulder the burden alone. As for Anne herself, she had had no opportunity to discover for herself what he thought. She had not seen him since they returned from Teotihuacán. He had thrown himself into his work as if to make up for the afternoon away from it. He did not breakfast at home, nor did he eat any other meal there. Sometimes Anne heard his car returning in the early hours of the morning and she would lie awake wondering where he had been and who had been with him. She had dreaded at first the thought of seeing him again after the discovery she had made about herself. But as the days passed, she grew restless, filled with an odd longing to be with him if only, she told herself, to test her reaction to his presence, to see if she could smile and talk and behave naturally. She had a terrible fear that she would give herself away in the first moment.

On the afternoon of the third day, Doña Isabel dismissed her. It had been a tiring morning, Anne, María, and the elderly woman had been closeted with the chef, though Anne, lost in a flood of Spanish and French, had retired to a corner while the final menu had been chosen. Fixing on a date had been equally exhausting, though they had finally settled on a week from Saturday. It had seemed a good choice to Anne. It would be two weeks to the day since she had come to Mexico. Her reign as Ramón's fiancée would be over. The night of the party, then, would be a perfect time to stage the scene that would put an end to this masquerade. No doubt that was what everyone would expect. It might be a good idea to discuss it with Ramón, if she could bring herself to broach the subject.

"Are you all right, my dear? You are looking very pale."

"I'm fine," Anne replied, flashing Doña Isabel a smile, "just thinking."

"I've kept you cooped up with me too long, I think. I'm a thoughtless old woman—and also an exhausted one. Why don't you run along, get out and get some air, while I indulge in a nap? It will do us both good."

Put like that, what else could she answer? Anne tried to make it clear that she enjoyed being useful, but she was quietly and firmly eased out of the room.

The house was quiet, echoing with emptiness in the warm, somnolent air. Nothing stirred. The rooms were spotless, the shuttered dimness filled with the smell of roses and beeswax. Luncheon was over, the preparations for dinner not yet begun. The servants were in their quarters resting. Anne knew that the most sensible thing she could do would be to follow their example, but she was too on edge to relax.

Moving as quietly as if she was afraid of being seen and stopped, she went to her room and found the small handbag Ramón had bought her, then slipped down the stairs and let herself out the front door. On one of the trips into the business district she had made with Doña Isabel she had cashed her salary check, taking most of it in traveler's checks but requesting a few Mexican pesos. It had given her an uncomfortably dependent feeling to have no money readily available to her, and she still had no idea when she would receive her payment from Ramón or what form it would take.

At the gate the keeper was nodding with his hat over his face as she slipped through. Outside, she stopped and took a deep breath, letting it out slowly. She had not realized how confined she had felt. She had not stirred a step in nearly a week without Ramón or Doña Isabel or some servant hovering. It was ridiculous to be so hemmed in, almost as if this was the nineteenth century and she an innocent Spanish maiden. It was odd how an attitude could linger long after the need of it had passed.

She walked along the street without considering where she was going or what she was going to do with her unexpected free time. The sun, warm on her hair, was kept from being too hot by a gentle breeze. Scents from hidden gardens teased her nostrils while the upper stories of ancient mansions stared down at her with hooded, indifferent eyes.

The residential street gave way to a busier thoroughfare. Nearby was a bus stop with a collection of people waiting around its bench: smiling women, most with net shopping bags on one arm and laughing, dark-eyed babies on the other; old men with fierce mustaches carrying canes; and ancient matrons in black, their hair covered and gloves on their hands against the strength of the sun. They were going downtown, most of them, she discovered. Every few minutes a bus would come by and pick up a half-dozen or so. By the time the next bus came more had gathered. Anne, more in curiosity than real intent to go shopping, joined the group. When a bus labeled Chapultepec Park pulled into the curb, she made a sudden decision and climbed on board.

Estela had mentioned the park in passing. It was supposed to be similar to Central Park in New York, a "fourteen hundred" acre area with walking and riding trails, a zoo, museums, lakes for boating, scenic trains, and a playground for smaller children. At the east end of the park on the high promontory known as Grasshopper Hill was Chapultepec Castle. The building once housed the West Point of Mexico and was the scene of the famous battle between the cadets and the U.S. Army during the Mexican War. At a later date the castle was the home of the ill-fated Emperor Maximilian and Empress Carlotta.

Anne walked slowly, idling through wooded glades and along avenues of ancient ahuehuete trees, massive giants that must have stood when Montezuma of the Aztecs was king. She stopped in the cool mist of the Aztec-style fountain, like a wall of water with the heads of feathered serpents protruding from the masonary. Moving on to the edge of the lake, she stood watching in amusement as the father of a young family tried to row a boat and at the same time keep three small, excited children, holding a balloon each, from overturning them all.

Time slipped past unnoticed. Tiring, she rested for a while in the convenient shade of a small pavillion with a domed roof and a platform protected by delicate wrought-iron grillwork. As the afternoon advanced, she slowly, surely, made her way toward Chapultepec Castle.

Being a week day, there were few people enjoying

the terraced, stone balustered gardens of the castle. The tiled walks under the airy arcades were deserted. Inside, the walls echoed to few footsteps other than her own, and there were only a few persons, including a pair of long-haired students with brown cigarettes burning between their fingers, standing before the fifty-foot-long mural by Juan O'Gorman. She recognized the style as being like the one on the wall in Ramón's library study. Anne stood staring at it a long time before moving on to the rooms used by Maximilian and his wife.

Once Anne had read a novel about Maximilian and his empress, Carlotta, who went slowly mad here in this place as her husband's fortunes in Mexico grew dim. It was easy to imagine her sweeping about this great stone pile overlooking the city, wringing her hands and weeping. Such thoughts combined with so much faded grandeur were depressing, and so she did not linger.

Below the castle was a museum, a fascinating collection of dioramas depicting the history of Mexico with emphasis on the fight for independence. Following the exhibits around the interior of the building, she emerged a full floor lower than when she had started.

She had gone perhaps a dozen yards beyond the museum when she glanced back to see the young men she had noticed at the castle leaving the museum behind her. A coincidence, she told herself and faced forward again, resolutely ignoring them. It was only because it was a long way back across the park and the hour was growing late that she quickened her step.

The path ahead of her branched and she took the right fork, hoping the young men would take the more direct route to the main entrance. They did not. Their footsteps rang hollowly behind her under the spreading branches of the tall ahuehuete trees.

No doubt they were going in that direction anyway; there was more than one entrance to the park. She must not panic. Even if this was a weekday instead of Sunday, when the park was crowded, even if this side path was becoming increasingly more wooded and remote from everything, there were bound to be people somewhere nearby. She could not come to any harm.

The footsteps were coming closer. Anne forced herself to walk on as if unaware. It was always possible the pair would pass her by. They were probably intent on their own business and it was only in her imagination that she was their quarry.

"Señorita!"

A brown hand with grime around the nails came out to catch her arm. Anne stopped. She wanted to fling off the hand that held her, but she was afraid it would start a struggle she could not win. Controlling a shiver, she stood still, her gaze raking the faces of the two young men. In their eyes was a caressing bravura backed by determination.

"What do you want?" she asked, forcing the words past her tight throat.

They looked taken aback at her English, but only for a moment. One of them said something in Spanish to the other and reached out to touch her tawny blond hair.

Anne jerked her head back. "Let me go," she said distinctly, glancing with purpose at the fingers still clutching her arm.

The two looked at each other, laughing, then eased closer.

Anne was as much angry as frightened. She thought she sensed a feeling of horseplay, of flirtatious amusement at her expense in their attitude. Still there was always the possibility that their intent could change.

"Touch me again and I'll scream," she warned them, flecks of gold sparkling in her brown eyes. Then as one of them began to snake an arm about her waist, she drew in her breath, preparing to put her threat into action.

A hint of something that was not amusement appeared in the face of the young man who held her arm. His grip tightened and his hand came up.

At that moment a sharp command rang out in Spanish. There was an instant of frozen stillness, then Anne found herself freed. As the young men stepped away from her, she swung to stare at the man approaching with the measured tread of anger from the direction they had come.

It was Ramón, his lips compressed into a thin line and his dark brows meeting together over his eyes. A few phrases more, and the two young men, their faces pale but impassive, muttered a few sentences that had the sound of an apology, then moved hurriedly on along the path.

Anne's smile as she turned from them was a little tremulous with relief. "Thank you," she said. "I don't know where you came from, but I was never so glad to see anyone in my life."

"I came from up at the castle. I saw you from the terrace," he said, his tone grim. "You are all right?"

"Oh, yes, I—I don't think they meant any harm."

"No, though most women object to being mauled." He took her elbow in a grip that was none too gentle, turning her toward the main gate.

"You think I don't," she said after a moment.

"Obviously not, or you would not have ignored my warning not to go out alone."

"I had no idea—" she began.

He cut across her protest. "Exactly, that is why you might have let yourself be guided by those who know."

Anne caught her breath. "In that case, all I can say is I am sorry to put you to the trouble of rescuing me."

He slanted her a dark look but made no reply for several steps. When Anne thought he did not intend to speak at all, he said, "If I had known you wanted to see the park I would have brought you."

"It—it was just an impulse," Anne said at last. "Besides, you have been so busy these last few days."

Ramón did not answer. The manner of their last parting hovered palpably between them. They walked in silence around the lake and back toward the gate through which Anne had entered. It was not until they were seated in Ramón's car that Anne was able to take a stab at normal conversation.

"How did you know where to find me?"

"One of the gardeners saw you leave the house. He followed you, saw you take the Chapultepec bus. He could not be easy in his mind until he told one of the maids, who told María, who informed my grandmother the moment she woke from her nap. Abuelita phoned me."

"I see," Anne said.

He sent her a sardonic look from the corner of his eye. "It is an ancient system of supervision, but a reliable one."

"I wonder," she said thoughtfully, "who it was designed to protect: your women or your men?"

She was a little afraid he might take offense, but he did not. "Does it matter," he asked, "as long as it works?"

"It makes unprotected women afraid and encourages the predatory instincts of men," she charged.

"I would have said it discouraged them," he answered dryly.

"It might discourage a man from paying his attentions to protected ones, but it gives him reason to think unprotected women are fair game."

"Aren't they?" he asked, taking his eyes from the traffic long enough to give her a smile. There was something so disturbing in it that she swallowed.

"Of course not. Every woman doesn't have a man to stand guard over her."

"She should have. Just as every man should have a woman to guard."

"But—but what of trust, and respect?"

"Agreeable virtues, both of them, among husbands and wives, but with strangers they do not prove reliable."

He meant not as reliable as the Spanish system of protection. "Watching your women, escorting them everywhere, following them about, it's archaic."

"Tried and true," he murmured, refusing to rise to provocation.

"It's changing all the time as more and more of your women find jobs and go out of the house to work."

"Perhaps," he said, inclining his head. "It won't change completely for some time, however, not in my generation, not in my house."

"How can you sit there—" she began, only to be interrupted.

"Tell me, what would you have done if I hadn't arrived when I did just now?"

"Screamed," she answered promptly.

"And then?"

"Fought" she said with less certainty.

"And after that?" When she did not answer, he went on. "Then you were as glad to see me as you said you were?"

"Yes—and I will admit that you are right in some ways. Still, there are few things so stifling as being overprotected. To escape it is worth some risk,"

His voice was grave when he answered, "I will try to remember that."

Ramón did not return to his office. After changing into an open-neck sports shirt, he ordered drinks served to Anne and himself on the patio and they sat outside in the gathering twilight. They did not talk much. There was a slight constraint between them, but not enough to compel Anne to break the companionable silence. She thought Ramón had something on his mind from the way he stared unseeing at the blue shadows beneath the arcade; she had no right to pry, however, and so sat mute.

It seemed that there were reminders of the brief nature of her stay in Mexico everywhere. If she had been Ramón's fiancée in truth, he might have shared his problem with her, asked her opinion on it. As things were, she could not expect that privilege.

Abruptly he turned to her in the dimness. "I had an invitation today from Irene. How would you feel about attending a costume party she is organizing for one of the local charities?"

"A costume party?"

"In a manner of speaking, an annual affair much to Irene's taste. The question is not whether you think it would be enjoyable, but if you feel up to courting another meeting with my cousin so soon? The date is set for next Thursday."

Thursday, only two days before their own party, two days before she must make her exit. She did not like the idea of sharing one of her last nights with Irene, still she could hardly say so.

"Do you want to go?" Anne asked, and found herself waiting without breathing for the answer.

"Not particularly. On the other hand, I wouldn't like to ignore what might be an olive branch."

Family ties were important to Ramón, to all of Mexican blood, she remembered Doña Isabel saying. Slowly she agreed.

"Still, there is something I don't quite trust about this invitation," he said meditatively.

"In what way?"

"It isn't like my dear cousin to forget a grievance so quickly, or to make the first move to heal a breach."

Anne would have liked to argue with that summation of Irene's character, but she did not quite dare. After a moment she asked, "What harm can there be in a party invitation?"

"None, I suppose. Perhaps it's just that she has a new man she wants to flaunt before me."

Was there a trace of bitterness in his voice? Anne could not decide.

"It might be best to give Irene the opportunity, then," she said, her tone expressionless.

"You think we should go?"

Anne avoided his eyes. "I see no reason why we shouldn't, if this is the kind of thing you would ordinarily attend with a fiancée."

"Very well. I will send our acceptance."

"What about costumes?"

"There's no need, a half-mask will do. Some few will wear costumes, most won't bother."

"That doesn't seem very festive. Why do they call it a costume party?"

He smiled at her mock disappointment. "It's a tradition for this particular charity," he said, mentioning an international organization.

"It—it is kind of Irene to become involved in such a worthy cause."

"Not at all. It is a matter of social prestige," he replied.

It was obvious, Anne, subsiding into silence once more, told herself, that he had few illusions concerning Irene. She must take what comfort she could from that.

Ramón, taking his responsibility seriously, went nowhere near the office that weekend. He dismissed his secretary until Monday morning, cleared the desk in his study, and put away his dark, conservative suits. On

Saturday morning he greeted Anne at the breakfast table in a cream-colored knit sports shirt worn with brown slacks.

Seating her in the chair across from his, he smiled into her wary eyes. "Behold me, your guide to Mexico. I am at your service, señorita. Where shall we go today?"

Anne, lowering her lashes, poured herself a cup of coffee before she answered. "You don't have to do this for my sake."

"I thought I had made my feelings on this subject plain," he said, taking his seat again and pushing his own cup toward her to be refilled. "I would rather you didn't go about alone, therefore I will go with you. It will give me great pleasure to show my city to you."

"Well then," she said with a sudden brilliant smile, "you had your chance to get out of it. I accept your generous offer."

"What would you like to see?" he inquired, settling back with a look of satisfaction.

"Everything," she declared. "Simply everything."

Despite an initial expression of comic dismay, Ramón obliged her. They visited the sixteenth-century cathedral, with its fourteen altars, in the center of the city; the nearby art museum in the Palacio de Bellas Artes, where they bought tickets for the much-discussed Ballet Folklórico; and then, as a change of pace, they strolled through the flower market on Luis Moya Street. He drove her out to the University of Mexico to view the famous mural-covered buildings; to his surprise, she recognized the work of Juan O'Gorman adorning the library building. From there they drove to the Basilica of Guadalupe, the shrine of the patron saint of Mexico.

On the way Ramón told her the legend of how it came to be built. The Virgin of Guadalupe was said to have appeared to a humble Indian in December of

1521, telling him of her desire to have a shrine erected
in her honor. The bishop to whom the Indian repeated
the request denied permission unless he received proof
of the visitation. The Virgin came once more to the
Indian and instructed him to take roses to the bishop
which he must pick from a barren rock. The Indian
found the roses where the Virgin indicated and placed
them under his cloak for safekeeping. When he
opened his cloak to present the flowers to the bishop,
there appeared on the inside of his cloak a painting of
the Virgin where the roses had been.

The "Dark Virgin" was much revered in Mexico and
her protection evoked on all occasions. When she saw
the painting Anne recognized her as the Virgin
represented in the small statuettes guarding taxicabs,
elevators, shops, and even street crossings, which she
had seen all over the city of Mexico. She was
impressed by the richness of the gold-and diamond-en-
crusted altar, endowed by those whom the Virgin had
helped, and the crutches, walking canes, and stretchers
left behind by her grateful worshipers.

Because of the crowd of pilgrims that came and
went on this weekend, they did not stay long, however.
They returned to the city in time to enjoy a leisurely
dinner at a restaurant, in the modern style, jutting out
over one of the lakes in Chapultepec Park.

Sunday was a family day. Estela and Esteban, with
their two children, descended on the house after early
Mass. Ramón's sister, in her vivacious way, was burst-
ing with ideas for their enjoyment. She had packed a
picnic, and after adding to it from the Castillo larder,
she swept them all off with her in Esteban's somewhat
dilapidated station wagon. Even Doña Isabel was included. Her cheeks pink with pleasure, the old lady
seemed content to share the third seat of the nine-pas-
senger vehicle with her great-grandchildren, a boy and
a girl.

They threaded the back roads of the city, arriving finally, as their first stop, at the Lagunilla Market. It was what Doña Isabel insisted on calling a thieves' market rather than a flea market. Wares of all kinds were displayed, from handicrafts to valuable antiques, in an open air shopping district which ran for blocks.

Estela, intent on finding a set of place mats of a particular shade of green, stopped before a straw weaver. Anne and Ramón, a solemn little girl of four with the impressive name of Consuelo swinging between their hands, walked on. Estela's children were impressively well-mannered, content to look without asking for all the pretty, bright-colored toys available. As a reward, Ramón, with a quick guilty glance at his sister, bought Consuelo a helium-filled balloon that he tied to her wrist to keep it from floating away. He also bought her a pink and yellow windmill on a stick, but found she could not hold it and his hand at the same time. He solved the problem by carrying it himself, as unselfconscious with that gaudy toy in his hand as if it had been a feathered scepter and he an Aztec king.

Consuelo was not the only one who received a gift. At a stall where antiques were laid out, tapestries and leather-bound books, silver plates and goblets and brass-bound chests, he began to bargain with the dealer. The piece that had caught his eye was a small, weathered wood statuette, about a foot high, of the Virgin of Guadalupe. She was represented wearing a crown in a blue cloak studded with stars over a garment of crimson and gold, her hands clasped and her faded features in dark wood were finely carved, investing her with an expression of understanding and serenity.

Anne could not be sure, but to her untutored eye the Virgin's crown looked overlaid with gold leaf and the raised stars of her cloak covered with sterling silver. She had little doubt that the statuette was of consider-

able value. When Ramón turned triumphant from his
bargaining session to present it to her, she could not
hide her dismay.

"She is beautiful, Ramón, truly beautiful, but I
couldn't take anything so valuable."

"You will have to, I've already bought her. And I
don't have another hand to hold her," he said, placing
the Virgin in the crook of Anne's arm and taking Consuelo's hand again, slipping the windmill from her fingers. The devil of laughter died away in his eyes as he
added, "Besides, I want you to have it. Call it a sou-
venir. Americans like to collect souvenirs of passing
pleasures, do they not?"

Anne turned sharply away as tears stung her eyes.
She made no further protests. Cradling the statuette
against her, holding Consuelo's hand, she walked on.

From the market they went to Xochimilco to enjoy
the famed floating gardens. They rented a gondola decorated with carnations and roses. Approximately
twenty-five feet long, it had railed sides and a curved
roof covering a long picnic table with benches on each
side. The boatman with his long pole stood at the
back. He was a friendly, indulgent man. A father himself, he had no objections to Consuelo and her older
brother, Juan, riding on the bench seat in the stern
where his own small boy sat beside him.

Moving gently over the water studded with lily pads
and water hyacinths, they ate their alfresco luncheon.
They washed down the cold chicken, meat-filled tor-
tillo's and fruit with cold drinks, beer and wine,
bought from a floating vendor. Then, serenaded by the
beautifully blending voices of a water-borne mariachi
band, cooled by a flower-scented breeze, they circum-
navigated the warm waters of the lake.

The Xochimilco Indians who entertained boatloads
of Mexicans and tourists each Sunday had been sup-
pliers of vegtables and flowers and fruits to the citizens

of Mexico City for centuries. Before the conquest, before Cortes was born, they had delivered their produce by canoe to the Venice-like city of the Aztec emperors, surrounded at that time by a network of canals. The land on which the Xochimilco lived was marshy, and so, to increase the yield of their crops, they built wooden rafts that they covered with soil and floated on the water. These were still in use, though the roots of the crops had long since extended down into the water, attaching the raft to the muddy bottom of the lakes and lagoons.

The produce of these floating gardens was hawked by canoe on Sunday also. Doña Isabel, seeing a vendor with his boat piled high with yellow dahlias, called him to the side of their gondola. What followed was a spirited bargaining session during which the vendor promised to deliver an enormous quantity of dahlias to the Castillo house on the morning of the party to supplement those ordered from the florist. The vendor accepted an offer for his flowers that was considerably less than he had wanted in the beginning. To console the poor man for being bested, Ramón bought the major part of his current cargo and distributed it among the ladies.

Anne smiled her thanks over the mass of perfect golden-yellow blooms. She could not speak. Consuelo, tired and full, finding her mother occupied with Doña Isabel in discussing plans for the party, had climbed into Anne's arms. She had gone to sleep there with the tender curve of her cheek pillowed against the softness of Ann's breast. To speak might awaken the little girl, and Anne found that she was reluctant to disturb her.

Her attention drawn by the bright picture Anne made under the shaded canopy of the gondola, Estela cast a sly smile at her brother.

"A golden madonna," she murmured, and looked

away to share with Doña Isabel a strange, almost secretive glance.

Ramón, reaching out to touch the hair of the sleeping child with gentle fingers, said nothing.

Chapter 7

On the following Monday Ramón returned to work. He was still able, however, to spare the time to show Anne around some of the late-closing museums and art galleries and to take her out to dinner. On Wednesday they attended the Ballet Folklórico as planned. Anne was enthralled with the pageantry, the beautifully authentic costumes, and the lilting music. The experience would always be one of her favorite memories of Mexico.

With Ramón at her side, protecting her from crowds and annoyance and language difficulties, explaining what she did not understand, she should have been completely happy. She was not. Though he was courteous and endlessly helpful, she had the feeling his attitude would have been the same if she had been his maiden aunt. When he touched her, it was in guidance or assistance; there was nothing personal in the contact. At the close of their outings together he escorted her punctiliously home and left her at the foot of the stairs.

Anne found his manner baffling. He seemed to enjoy her company, he took meticulous pains to ensure her pleasure, but he never took her in his arms, never kissed her. Sometimes she could not help but think his restraint unnatural, a penance self-imposed. At others she was forced to wonder if she no longer held any interest for him.

As the days passed, the date of Irene's party drew relentlessly nearer. Doña Isabel when she learned of the gala her great-niece had planned, was not at all pleased.

"I do not like it. Mark my words, she has some devious scheme in mind to take the shine from our own party. Why in the name of all the saints didn't you refuse to go when you had the chance, my dear Anne?"

"I didn't feel I had the right," Anne tried to explain.

"Right? Pray, what does that mean? You are the fiancée of Ramón Carlos Castillo, are you not? You are the injured party, the person who was insulted by this woman. Who has a better right?"

"But you know—" Anne began, only to be waved into silence.

"Never mind. It is done now. We must make the best of it."

"You will go too?" Anne asked.

"I'm not sure. It is certain to be an overcrowded affair with a lot of loud noise called music and a too generous supply of drink. It has been some time since such a gathering was to my taste. You and Ramón can be representatives for the Castillo family, and I expect Estela and Esteban will put in an appearance. That should be enough."

"I could do with your moral support," Anne told the elderly woman with a smile.

"Moral support you shall have, though it may come from another source," Doña Isabel said, winking.

It was during the afternoon two days later, before Anne discovered what the old lady meant. Calling for the car, Doña Isabel took Anne into town to her favorite hairdresser. After listening closely to his elderly customer, the hairdresser had shampooed Anne's hair and set it. When it was dry, he swept it into a mass of loose, shining curls at the back of her head. Soft tendrils were teased forward to curl before her ears. That done, she received the first professional manicure of her life, though her nails, after being shaped, were buffed to a high gloss rather than polished. Makeup came next, a skillful blending made her eyes appear enormous in her pale face and caused her lips to glisten with the pink and dewy innocence of childhood. The effect was topped off by a final complimentary spray of some perfume that had the sweet seductiveness of roses and gardenias.

Though Doña Isabel heaped praises on her hairdresser for the effect he and his beauticians had achieved, she did not stop there. Anne had expected to wear the last of the dresses Ramón had bought for her, the long gown of salmon and rust. Instead, she found a creation far different laid out upon her bed when she returned. There was no card, no message with it, but it was such a perfect foil for the hairstyle she had been given that Anne did not doubt for a moment Ramón's grandmother had had it delivered for her.

Anne was not very knowledgeable about Mexican native costume; still, even she could recognize that style in the superb dress she had been given. It consisted of a double skirt, one longer by at least a foot than the other. The top skirt was of maroon velvet, banded and fringed with gold, to be worn over a petticoat of lace ending in a deep lace flounce. The topskirt had side slits edged with gold bands and tied up with maroon and pink ribbons. With this went a soft white blouse stiff about the neck and sleeves with embroidery, and, to be worn over that, a short vest of maroon satin embroidered with gold and tied over the breast with ribbons. Also included was a long satin sash trimmed on the ends with gold fringe, and a pair of satin slippers embroidered on the toe.

Bathing while trying to keep her hair from getting damp or smudging her makeup was not very relaxing;

Anne did not linger over it. Anxious to try the dress for fit, she put it on at once.

When the last ribbon was tied, she turned to look in the mirror. The fit was perfect, the skirt length fine with the low-heeled slippers, still, she felt a twinge of disquiet. The color was rich, even becoming, but she had to admit that it was also a little garish, expecially with the intense pink of the ribbons. The style, though it might have been carried off by a brunette, had a tendency to overwhelm her subdued blond coloring.

Still, she could not disappoint Doña Isabel. She had to wear the dress.

Estela and Esteban had accepted the invitation and it had been decided they would all go together. Ramón's sister and her husband had already arrived at the house when Anne came down. She could hear them laughing and talking above Ramón's deeper tones from the direction of the sala as she descended the stairs.

There was no one in the hall. She hesitated on the bottom step, thinking that she should go to Doña Isabel first to thank her for her gift of the costume. The old lady might be waiting to see her in it. She would be anxious to check her final donation to the proceedings since she had decided against putting in an appearance herself.

As she wavered there, Estela came out of the sala, throwing a last bit of repartee over her shoulder. She was dressed in a knee-length dress composed of white flounces edged in red for a picotee effect. With red spaghetti-strap sandals, she looked charmingly cosmopolitan. Then as she saw Anne, the blood drained from her face, leaving it as white as the flounces of her dress.

Her sudden stillness alerted the two men. They came to the door of the room. Esteban glanced at his wife in puzzlement, flashing Anne his easy, friendly smile. But on Ramón the effect was the same as on his sister.

As the stunned silence continued without end, Esteban stepped forward. "Good evening, Anne," he said, clearing his throat. "I hope—that is—I trust nothing is wrong?"

Estela found her voice at last. "That dress—" she said. "Where did you get it?"

"It was in my room, laid out for me to wear," Anne answered over the tightness in her throat. "What is it? What's the matter?"

"You will go upstairs and take it off," Ramón told her, an accusation she could not understand burning with the cold fury in his eyes.

"Take it off?" she repeated without comprehension. "But what shall I wear?"

Moving to the foot of the stairs with a noiseless tread that somehow signaled danger, he answered. "Wear the turquoise, wear anything, but take that dress off."

The softness of his tone sent a shiver of alarm along her veins. "Why? I don't understand," she cried.

"It doesn't matter why," he said in a voice low enough to be heard by Anne alone. "If you don't go upstairs and remove it immediately, I am going to carry you there and tear it off myself!"

There could be little doubt he meant what he said. In his quiet tone was a steely determination that brooked no refusal. Still Anne wavered. It was such a senseless fuss over nothing that she could see. She wanted only some reason for the violence of their reaction. It did not seem too much to ask.

As she stood without moving, the maroon and pink ribbons across her breast rising and falling with the quickness of her breathing, Ramón's hand tightened on the stair rail until the knuckles showed white. An explosive tension filled the air. Anne found she could

not look away from the harsh, commanding light in
Ramón's dark eyes.

It was Estela who shattered the strained tableau.
Stepping forward with her small hands clasped and an
appeal in her wide black eyes, she said, "Shall I go
with you? If I help you to change, it won't take long."

The offer was the deciding factor. With no more
than a nod, Anne turned and, with Ramón's sister
beside her, ascended the stairs once more.

They moved along the hall in silence. Anne opened
her bedroom door and allowed Estela to precede her.

The other girl glanced at the gold-stamped white
dress box, still lying on the floor beside the wastepaper
basket, in which the costume had arrived. Without
comment, she moved to the wardrobe, from which she
took out the turquoise dress and spread it with care
over the bed. She stood fingering the iridescent blue
and green material thoughtfully for a moment before
she took a deep breath, squared her shoulders, and
looked at Anne.

"You must forgive Ramón, really you must. He has
reason for his attitude."

Anne stripped off the velvet vest of her costume and
tossed it on the bed. "Does he?" she asked without inflection.

"Yes," Estela asserted, flicking the ribbons of the
vest with a disdainful gaze. "You see, this dress you are
wearing is of the *poblana*, the women of the Pueblo.
They are traditionally beautiful, but of few morals and
many vices. You comprehend?"

"I see," Anne replied slowly as with fingers grown
suddenly clumsy she untied the fringed sash about her
waist.

"That is not all," Estela went on with a lift of her
chin. "Ramón would be very angry if he knew what I
am about to tell you, but I think that it is important
for you to understand his feelings."

"If he would not like it—" Anne began, but Estela waved her compunction away with a quick gesture. As if agitated by her thoughts, she moved to the window, staring out.

"Our mother—but perhaps someone, Abuelita even, had told you about the woman who was the mother of Ramón and myself?"

Anne shook her head. "Doña Isabel spoke of your father and his death. She did not mention your mother."

"No, she would not. It is not a part of her life she likes to remember. Our mother, you see, was an American movie actress—not, it must be admitted, a very good one. Our father, rich, handsome, and also young and impressionable, was visiting in California when they met. Our mother was a beautiful woman, as fair as our father was dark, but cold and calculating. She managed to give the impression that she might warm to life for the right man. Realizing that her career as an actress was at a standstill, she turned her attention to the young Mexican millionaire. She thought she would be rich, cosseted by a husband she could manipulate at will. It was a dreadful mistake. Our father was not so easily led as she imagined. He had certain standards he expected her to meet, certain obligations he expected her to fulfill. For some years the feuding was confined to the family, but eventually the warfare became an open secret."

Stepping out of the skirt of her costume, Anne tossed it aside with the blouse and slipped the turquoise dress on over her head, settling it into place. The picture Estela had painted for her was clear. It explained many things she had not understood. Ramón's immediate distrust of her as an American, his excessive contempt for women who chased after him for his money.

Estela, turning from the window in time to help
Anne with the zipper of her dress, went on.

"As was natural, they came to hate each other, both
feeling they had been duped. The woman our father
had married made little attempt to fit into his life. She
went her own way, flaunting custom and tradition. She
scorned Mexican society and made her friends among
the raffish and seamy underworld of the city, the Bohe-
mian element my father could only despise.

"Somehow she learned that the dress of the *poblana*
was frowned upon by good society and she made a
point of wearing it, deliberately provoking our father
and society. And there was a certain justness in the action, for at this time she was having an affair with her
husband's cousin and best friend, a married man,
Irene's father. The two of them, our mother and her
lover, went away together to the west coast to Acapulco, where he kept a yacht. My father followed. We
heard later there had been a boating accident. None of
them returned."

Anne drew in her breath. "I think I see why you and
Ramón were so upset."

"Yes," Estela said, her lips twisting in a hard smile.
"It leaps to the eye also then the reason why the dress
was sent. Someone wanted to remind Ramón that you
are of the same nationality as his mother, and perhaps
of the same disposition. Who else could that someone
be except Irene?"

Irene, not Doña Isabela, had sent the dress. Yes, it
made sense that she would do such a thing. And because of the way Anne and Ramón had met, the plan
was more effective than Irene could have imagined. It
was a pity, then, that the Mexican girl had not known
there was no need for such drastic measures.

"I am glad you told me," Anne said simply.

"So am I," Estela replied, smiling as she touched
Anne's hand lightly.

Returning the smile a little wearily, Anne turned to the mirror of the dressing table, checking to see that she had not disarranged her hair. She was pale, too pale; the cherry lip gloss she had applied earlier to suit the maroon costume standing out like blood on her lips.

With hands that trembled slightly she picked up the heart-shaped turquoise pendant that lay on the polished surface of the table. She placed it over her head so that it hung, a cold, lifeless weight, between her breasts. But it was no more lifeless than the heart that beat beneath it.

"I suppose I should do something about my make-up," she said in a voice as normal as she could make it.

Estela hesitated a moment, a thoughtful look in her bright eyes, before moving to the door.

"I will wait for you downstairs then," she replied. Flashing a smile that was meant to be encouraging, she slipped out of the room.

Anne was grateful for the other girl's support, but she also appreciated her tact in leaving her alone for a few minutes. She needed some time to herself. Time to come to grips with what she had learned.

To discover that another person, someone she hardly knew, someone she had not personally harmed, wished to humiliate and hurt her was a shock. There were, however, worse things. For instance, the discovery that somewhere deep in the recesses of her mind she had cherished the small, secret hope that this mock engagement might eventually become real.

It was foolish but nonetheless true.

How she had come to allow such a slim hope to take root she could not imagine, still she must face the fact that it could never be. Ramón Castillo might have felt some brief, easily controlled attraction to her once or twice, but he had made how he felt about the kind of woman he considered her to be very plain. His prejudice against her was no millionaire's whim, no mere aversion to being pursued. To him she represented everything he despised. She was fair; she had, or so he thought, forced herself on him; and finally she, like his mother, had worn the dress of the poblana, mocking the traditions of his country.

No, it was too much to believe that he could overcome so strong a prejudice for her sake. It was even more ridiculous to think that he might wish to try.

With fingers that trembled, she took up a tissue and wiped the color from her mouth. Steadying her hand, she applied a film of pale-pink gloss. With bleak eyes, she studied the effect, her mind far from what she was doing.

Soon, too soon, her days in Mexico would be over. She would go home, back to the apartment she shared with Judy, back to Joe and Iva, and to Metcalf's. Not so long ago, the prospect had seemed all she could wish. It had represented everything dear and familiar and secure. Now this room, this house, the color and the flowers the radiant sun and pure light of Mexico, seemed a part of her, a link to the dark, enigmatic man she had come to love, The prospect of leaving, returning to Dallas and all she had left, had the feeling of dreary exile.

Chapter 8

The ride to the hotel where the charity gala was to be held was the longest Anne had ever endured. She and Ramón had not spoken, though he had given a short nod of approval of her appearance when she rejoined them before setting out. Estela and Esteban had gone on ahead. They could have fitted with ease into the chauffeur-driven limousine, but Estela declared she intended to leave early even if she had to plead the responsibilities of motherhood as an excuse.

Ramón's sister appeared to have thrown off her agitation and concern for a lighter mood. Ramón had not. He sat in the corner, one elbow on the armrest, pulling at his lower lip, as was his habit while thinking. He stared broodingly out the window, his face lit by the intermittent glow of passing streetlights.

Anne unconsciously copied his attitude. Her attention was caught by a flash of what she thought was lightning over the mountains. The night lights of the city, the enclosing buildings, made it difficult to be certain, but she thought it was darker than was usual at this altitude, and there was a sultry feeling of an impending storm in the air.

The glass separating them from their driver was up. Leaning forward, Ramón pressed the button for the intercom system and gave an order. The chauffeur immediately pulled over to the curb. Anne glanced at Ramón in surprise. They were near the heart of the city, but the building they had come to a halt in in front of was not the hotel Irene had named in her invitation.

"Why are we stopping?" Anne asked.

He did not give a direct answer. "Estela tells me the dress you were wearing tonight was delivered to your room. According to the servants, it arrived by special messenger late this afternoon. The box in which it was packed Estela recognized as coming from Irene's favorite dress shop."

Estela had not mentioned the dress box to her, but Anne was glad of that small bit of corroborating evidence. She nodded.

His voice tight with suppressed anger, he went on. "I should have recognized her fine hand in the choice. I acted without thought. My apologies to you for the embarrassment I caused you."

"That's all right," Anne managed to answer. "I'm sure you had your reasons."

He flicked a hard glance in her direction, but did not comment. He said instead, "The question now is, what are we going to do about it?"

"I— What do you mean?"

"Are we going to allow Irene the satisfaction of thinking that her little stratagem was successful? I find that thought hard to bear."

Anne could easily see his point. "What are you suggesting?"

"Irene hoped to cause a rift between us. She hoped to see you wear the gown in defiance, as my mother would have done, possibly to see me grim and silent, a man whose eyes had been opened. Failing that, she will expect that we will at least be at odds with each other over the question of what you are wearing. I propose only to disappoint her."

"In what way?" Anne asked, though she thought she could guess.

"By acting the exact opposite of what she expects, of course. Need I spell it out?"

"I'm— no, I suppose not."

"Well, then? Are we agreed?"

Could she bear to smile and laugh, to dance and feel his arms around her, to return his possessive and intimate glances? She must, whatever the cost.

Perhaps it might be endurable if she could pretend it was a game, a sporting contest between rivals. She against Irene—though there would be no prize awarded.

"Agreed," she said, her voice husky as she gave him her hand.

The first test of their pact came the moment they stepped into the ballroom of the hotel. Irene, scintillating in a long dress of black covered with gold sequins and a headdress topped by a feather plume to match, hurried forward to greet them.

"Ramón," she exclaimed, her voice pitched so high with excitement that heads turned in their direction from all around. "I'm so glad you could come, but you haven't worn a costume, you devil, you or your charming fiancée. I suppose I must forgive you, however. When could I ever do otherwise?"

She clutched Ramón's arm, an arch look in her eyes. She drank in his calm greeting before turning her bright, malicious gaze on Anne.

"My dear Miss . . . Mathews . . . was it not? You look darling in your little turquoise number, but then, you always do."

The sly reference to the fact that Irene had seen her wearing the turquoise gown before was not lost on Anne.

"Why, thank you," she said, smiling. Complacently, almost possessively, she placed her left hand over her right where it was tucked into the crook of Ramón's other arm. "I love wearing it because Ramón bought it for me. I had nothing with me on this visit to use as a costume, but I thought this dress might pass muster since Ramón told me once that in it I reminded him of the Aztec rain goddess, Our Lady of the Turquoise Skirt."

The gasp Irene gave was plainly audible. In the sudden silence could be heard a titter of laughter at the woman's expense, quickly stifled. Anne was aware of the tightening of the muscles of Ramón's arm, a small signal of approval and congratulations.

His manner perfectly easy, he filled the awkward moment with a few words of commendation to Irene for her charity work and the splendor of the decorations for the occasion. Detaching himself from her nerveless grasp, he declined to be so selfish as to keep her from her other guests. Before she could recover they made their escape.

Shortly afterward, they were joined by Estela and Esteban, and the four of them found a table far enough from the musicians for comfortable conversation. Several couples stopped by to greet them and were introduced. Their attitude was cordial, faintly tinged with curiosity.

Anne and Ramón danced a number of times. Once Anne felt his lips brush her hair and another time the skin of her neck below her ear, but when she drew back to look at him, he merely returned her gaze with the lift of an eyebrow as though it had been no more than a part of the act. They varied this performance by conducting conversations of absorbing interest concerning the different people in the room who were Ramón's friends and acquaintances and by smiling with apparent delight in each other's company.

Once or twice they changed partners with Estela and Esteban. Anne found she liked Estela's quiet, bearded husband more each time they met. Whether he had been primed by his wife on the way to the hotel, or from an innate politeness, he asked no awkward questions. He talked to her of her home state, Texas, of the worthiness of the charity the gala honored, and when the subject turned to the weather, he gave it as his grave and most considered opinion that a storm was due to break over the city before morning. The rainy season was not due for some months yet, but the weather had held too good for too long.

The night wore on. The heaviness in the air seemed to increase, though it was impossible for them to hear the sound of thunder over the beat of the music or the laughter and chatter of the crowd.

A champagne supper served from long tables decorated with ice sculptures presented another opportunity for Anne and Ramón to display their solidarity. They made a great show of serving each other's plates and recommending the delicacies they had sampled to each other. Still, keeping up such a pretense at lightheartedness proved an effort for Anne. The glass of champagne she drank did nothing to ease the pressure gradually gathering behind her eyes, caused by strain and the sullen atmosphere. If anything, it made it worse.

Supper had not been long over when Estela and Esteban deserted them, leaving the party. Soon afterward Irene approached their table with a rather embarrassed-looking young man in tow. It became obvious that he had been commandeered for the express purpose of asking Anne to dance, leaving Ramón free to partner Irene.

Short of actual rudeness, there seemed no way to refuse.

The young man, as if determined to make his sacrifice complete, kept up a barrage of questions: How did she like Mexico? Would she be staying long? What had she seen? Which did she like best? It might have been more flattering if he had not kept glancing around, trying to keep an eye on Irene as she danced with Ramón. Anne thought he was relieved when she pleaded a headache and asked him to get her something to drink.

Anne found that she herself derived no pleasure from watching Ramón with the Mexican woman. As soon as her own dancing partner was out of sight, she slipped away, going in search of the quiet of the ladies' powder room and lounge.

The headache was not a fiction. By now it was only too real. She was able to get a pain tablet and a paper cup full of water from the maid on duty in the powder room. Swallowing it, she retreated to a small brocaded settee in the lounge. For the moment she had the room to herself and she leaned back, closing her eyes, trying to relax.

In her mind's eye she could see Irene moving into Ramón's arms, her head thrown back and a rapt expression in her narrow brown eyes. Despite the woman's personality, despite what she had tried to do, there could be no doubt that she cared for Ramón. With the same nationality as his, the same language and customs and circle of friends, there could be little doubt also that she would make him a suitable wife. If she was strong-willed, well, so was he. She would not disgrace him by wearing the wrong clothes or choosing the wrong set of friends. Mingling his blood with hers would help to obliterate the American strain in his bloodline, which he so despised. Their children . . .

"So!" This is where you have hidden yourself away."

Startled, Anne opened her eyes to find Irene standing in the lounge doorway. The Mexican girl let the heavy panel fall shut and sauntered toward her.

"You will be happy to know, Señorita Matthews, that Ramón is looking for you. He sent me—me!—as a messenger to tell you he is ready to leave. But first there is something we must discuss, you and I."

Anne got to her feet. Looking around for a waste

basket, she disposed of the paper cup she still held. "I know of nothing," she said.

Stepping around the other girl, she moved toward the door.

Irene swung around, her voice rising. "Don't you? Don't you indeed! Well, that's too bad. I have something to say to you concerning this marriage, and you will listen."

Anne pushed open the door. "I think not," she said softly and went out, letting it fall to behind her.

She had not gone more than a step before the other girl came catapulting out of the lounge.

"And I say yes, you will listen!" she screamed. "You stupid little fool, what do you know of love, or of the deep passions of our race? What do you have to give a man like Ramón Castillo? There is no fire under your sweet paleness; you will bore him within a year. And then what? Your face will mock him with memories of his mother's disgrace. You will find no happiness because he will have none. What good will all his money do you when you find your husband hates you? What can you do, except look elsewhere and bring scandal and tragedy down upon the Castillo house once more, as did that other pale American, his mother? We have long memories here in Mexico. Everywhere you look you will find someone who knows who you are, and what happened to one of your kind in the past. And so everywhere you will find your future, waiting."

Frowning, Anne said slowly, "The future is fresh and new—it does not depend on the past. But I wonder how much you and your kind, with your pessimism and disapproving faces and dire warnings had to do with what happened to Ramón's mother. There is also this: A woman pressured and scorned on all sides may have an affair, but she does not have one alone. There is always a man in it somewhere who must share the blame."

Her face contorted, Irene cried, "My father was not to blame! He was a victim of that she-devil!"

"Oh yes! A victim who was, of course, lured aboard his own yacht at Acapulco?"

"How dare you!" she shouted, her eyes blazing and her fingers curling into claws as she advanced on Anne. "How dare you suggest such a thing!"

The need to strike out at her was plain in every line of Irene's body. Anne stood her ground, determined not to flinch or move. What she had said was no more than the truth and she would retract not a word of it.

Just as Irene reached her, a man moved from the outer hallway to stand quietly at Anne's side.

The Mexican woman halted as if she had stepped into an electric fence.

"I can see you delivered my message, Irene," Ramón said, irony lacing his even tone. "My thanks. Anne, darling, are you ready to leave?"

"Yes, Yes, I am, " Anne answered dazedly, as she felt his fingers warm and firm at her elbow.

"Then all that remains is to pay our respects to our hostess and go." With a nod in Irene's direction that was considerably less polite than his tone, he swung around, and with Anne beside him, walked away.

A gust of wind lifted the tendrils of hair about Anne's face as she stepped out of the car onto the front drive. The Castillo house loomed large and dark before them, shadows moving under the entrance arcade as the wrought-iron lantern left alight there swayed in the wind.

Anne shivered a little as she passed before Ramón into the house. It was not the tension of the impending storm which gripped her, however, but something far different. Ramón had said almost nothing on the drive home. How much he had overheard of the conversation with Irene she could not tell; she suspected it was no small amount. She had waited for him to make some comment, but he had not. She would almost have preferred him to lash out at her, condemning her for discussing his private affairs, for giving her opinion on matters which she was ill prepared to judge. Anything would have been better than the endless, nerve-wracking quiet.

The stained-glass lantern sprang to life in the entrance hall. Tonight there was no María waiting up for them; she had given up her mightly vigils in the last few days.

Ramón locked the front door behind them, then paused with his hand on the light switch, looking up at Anne who was already halfway up the stairs.

"Would you like a cup of coffee?" he asked. "I gave orders to have a percolator left ready in the library."

Anne retraced her steps with a certain wariness. The coffee sounded lovely—it was the purpose behind it which troubled her.

In the study Ramón plugged in the coffee pot. There was only one cup and saucer on the tray, so while it heated he went to find another.

Anne moved to the French window at the far end of the room and, pulling aside the heavy drapes, looked out. The library was one of the rooms which opened out onto the central patio. The center square was dark and still within the protecting walls—then, as she watched, lightning flared. For a blinding instant it filled the patio with a yellow-blue glow, outlining the leaves of plants and trees and the forms of containers and statues with cool fire. Thunder, deadened by the thick walls of the house, followed within seconds. As if touched off in some way by the lightning, a reckless excitement gripped her. She could not possibly sleep in this kind of weather. Her headache was gone. Why shouldn't she grasp at the last few hours remaining to her with the man she loved? What did it matter what he said to her? He did not realize the power he had to hurt her, nor would she allow him to guess at it, whatever he chose to accuse her of. And why shouldn't she say what she pleased also? She had no reason to fear physical retaliation. To be banished would be the worst punishment, and one she must endure anyway. When she was gone, nothing she had said would make any difference.

When Ramón entered the room she dropped the drape and turned with a smile. He placed the cup and saucer on the tray, then stood with one hand resting on the desk.

"I believe that I am indebted to you," he said quietly.

Anne's smile faded. "Indebted?" she said without comprehension.

"For defending my mother to Irene—and, just possibly, giving me a new slant on what I had been taught to think of as solely my mother's indiscretions."

It was the one reaction she had not considered. "I'm sorry if I interfered in something that was none of my business."

"I imagine Estela told you?"

Anne nodded. "She seemed to think I had a right to know. Under the circumstances I could hardly tell her differently."

"No, and I doubt if Irene gave you much more opportunity to deny any interest."

Again she agreed with a shake of her head.

"You see? I'm not an unreasonable man. As I told you, I'm grateful for it. I have always been led to believe, you know, that my mother was in the wrong in what she did, and my father completely in the right. It never occurred to me to question it, I'm ashamed to say. There is always the possibility that the version I was given was the correct one—but at least I will no longer condemn the woman who bore me without an attempt to discover the facts. I owe her that much."

"I'm glad," Anne said simply.

"Because she was an American?" he asked with the lift of a sardonic eyebrow.

Shielding her expression with her lashes she answered, "Not entirely, although I suppose that is part of it."

"And the rest."

"I think," Anne said slowly, "that I feel a certain—kinship—with her. Our circumstances were not the same, of course," she went on quickly, "but I think I can understand how she must have felt, alone here, without friends or relatives, tied to a man she did not love."

A stiffness settled over Ramón's features. "Yes," he said; "even I can see how that might make a difference."

The bubbling noise of the coffee pot provided a distraction. Seeing that the coffee was ready, Anne moved to pour out the steaming brew. Ramón took the cup she handed him with a preoccupied air, as if he had forgotten that it was the main purpose for their being there.

As Anne took up her own cup, lightning flashed once more outside the window. As if drawn by the flickering light, Ramón pushed open the French window and stepped outside, his cup in his hand.

The cool wind which swept into the room carried the damp earth smell of coming rain and brought the sound of thunder nearer. Anne could not resist following Ramón out into the darkness of the overhanging loggia. Another pulsing flash of lightning picked out his tall shape leaning against one of the stone columns. It seemed natural to settle against the next in line. In silence that was neither easy nor uneasy, they stood drinking their coffee, staring out into the tumultuous blackness of the night.

At last Ramón spoke. "So you think my mother made a bad bargain?"

"It would seem so," she replied.

"Not even a millionaire's wealth could make living in this country bearable?"

"Mexico is a beautiful country. It could be a wonderful place to live, if two people loved each other. If they didn't, all the money in the world couldn't make them happy together, here or anywhere else."

Her voice carried a strong note of defiance because she knew he thought of her as a gold-digger, but he did not take up the challenge. His face in a blue-white glitter of lightning looked pale and bleak.

Lost in thought, her eyes dazzled by the bright glow and the mutter of thunder in her ears, Anne was not aware Ramón had moved until he loomed up beside her. He took the empty coffee cup from her hand and placed it with his own in a nearby stone trough filled with pansies. When his arms closed around her, a shiver of surprise and abrupt awareness of the chill in the air caught her and then his lips, bitter-sweet with the taste of coffee, were on hers. He teased her mouth with gentle, experimental kisses, trailing fire across the curve of her cheek to her hairline. His arms tightened, his hands moved over her back, drawing her closer against him. "Anne," he murmured, his voice low and husky, his breath warm against her neck. "*Por Dios*, I want you so."

She tried to speak his name but his mouth captured her parted lips as he crushed her to him. His fingers cupped her chin, dropping to the tender hollow of her throat, then to the soft curves beneath the smooth silk of her bodice.

"I thought I could keep away from you, but I cannot. Somehow you have crept into my brain and my blood. Stay with me, Anne, *mi alma*. I will give you anything you ask, only stay with me."

He had spoken no word of love. He had said he wanted her, no more than that. And in return he was prepared to give her anything she wanted—except himself. Despite everything she had said, he was offering to bribe her with his money! It should have been funny, that he would offer the one thing he had so despised the other women he had known for finding attractive. It was not. It was only painful that he could still think she would accept such an offer.

"Ramón—" she said, her breath catching on the pain caused by speaking his name. Tears that seemed to rise upward from her heart crowded into her throat.

"Yes, querida?"

"Please," she whispered, pressing her hands against his chest.

The muscles of his arms were steely with resistance. Beneath her fingers she could feel the heavy beating of his heart and the abrupt cessation of his breathing. Suddenly she was free.

An absurd feeling that she should apologize touched her. She wished she could see his face instead of the dark, shadowed silhouette he presented in the faint light from the library.

Without warning the tension within her snapped. She whirled, pushing through the French window into the house. She thought she heard him call her name, but she did not stop. She could not. She had to reach her room before the blinding tears came and she could not find her way.

Chapter 9

The day of the engagement party dawned bright and clear and continued unclouded. It was a good omen, Doña Isabel insisted. Anne, staring without seeing out into the waning yellow light of late afternoon, was unconvinced. What she was still doing at the Castillo house she could not fully understand. Her first impulse had been to run away in the middle of the night. Only the knowledge that she was unlikely to be able to complete her escape without detection had deterred her. How ignominious it would have been to be stopped by the housekeeper or have one of the gardeners send Ramón after her again!

Morning had brought a calmer frame of mind. She had an obligation to fulfill. She was helped to keep to this purpose by the discovery that Ramón had already left for his office and would not be back until dinner time. It occurred to her that he might want to avoid her as much as she wanted to avoid him. If so, then the two days and nights that remained before she could consider herself released might be got through without too much embarrassment to either of them.

So it had proved. On Friday Ramón had not returned to the house until well after midnight. Lying awake, Anne had heard his car pull up before the front door. When she drew aside the drapes to glance out the window, she thought he looked tired. The weariness of his movements as he slung his sports coat over his shoulder and rubbed a hand over his head to the back of his neck made her wince as though she had touched a tender nerve.

The next morning she ate a working breakfast with Doña Isabel in her room. During the course of the meal she took two pages of notes concerning the last-minute details to make the house ready for the party. She was kept so busy seeing to them for the rest of the day that she did not have time to worry that he might meet Ramón around any corner. She was not even sure that he was in the house.

But at last everything was ready. The reception rooms were immaculate. The monogrammed napkins, the polished glasses, the fruits and nuts and bonbons, were laid out upon the highly waxed tables. The flower arrangements of dahlias and roses graced with fern and baby's breath scented the air. The lights were discreetly lowered and candles supported in holders of silver and crystal placed here and there, waiting to be lit. The caterers had taken over the kitchen, where it was now their responsibility to worry about the supply of ice and the amount of liquid refreshment. Soon daylight would fade, the time would draw near, the maid stationed below in the hall would begin to take the hats and coats of the arriving guests. Soon, a matter of hours, it would be over.

"Is something troubling you, my dear?" Doña Isabel inquired softly.

Summoning a smile, Anne turned from the window. "No, I'm fine."

Doña Isabel sat in her dressing gown of lavender velvet. Her hair had been dressed in shining silver curls. She had only to ring for Maria to help her slip on her dress to be ready to go downstairs.

"You have been with us two weeks now, have you

not?" she asked, tilting her head on one side, a far too knowing look in her fine old eyes.

"Two weeks today," Anne agreed.

"You would not be thinking of leaving?"

"I—think I must."

"Why?" the old lady asked in a tone of perfect reason. "What does it matter, two weeks, three, four, a month?"

"My job," Anne began.

"I'm sure they could release you if you asked. Your friends, the Metcalfs, sound like reasonable people who would wish you to take advantage of your opportunities."

"You know my agreement with Ramón called for only two weeks," Anne protested, though she could not help smiling at the cajoling tone Doña Isabel had chosen to take.

The old lady compressed her lips. "I suppose I am a selfish old woman, but I find I cannot do without you. I see I will have to talk to my grandson."

Alarmed, Anne exclaimed, "Don't do that!"

A pucker appeared in the crepe-like skin of her forehead. "Of course, if you don't wish to stay . . ."

"It isn't that," Anne said miserably. "If things were different, I could stay here with pleasure forever, but as they stand it's impossible."

"I see. Am I to understand that you have quarreled with my grandson?"

"Not exactly."

"It is still your disagreement over Irene's ill-natured trick with the *poblana* dress?"

Anne shook her head.

"Am I to take it then that Ramón has behaved in a manner you find objectionable?" Doña Isabel persisted, the frown deepening into two sharp lines between her eyes. "If so, then I know I will speak to him."

The thought of the indomitable old lady tackling

her grandson, a man well over thirty, on such a delicate subject might at any other time have been amusing. As it was, Anne was horrified. "No, please! I just—I just want to return home. That's all!"

Doña Isabel stared at her a long moment. "You do not intend to come back?"

"I—no."

To speak that one small word was one of the hardest things Anne had ever done. She looked away from the old woman to hide the tears that rose into her eyes.

"I see," Doña Isabel sighed. "Perhaps you are wise, I don't know. I do know that I am sorry for it. I have met many Americans. Some I have liked, some not. I did not like the woman who was Ramón's mother. It was an instinctive thing, felt at the first meeting—perhaps a regrettable thing, but it could not be helped. Just as I could not help the instinct I felt when I first saw you standing so pale and ill in the hall outside. I knew we would be friends; I felt, I hoped, that we might be even closer. These things are as God wills."

"Doña Isabel . . ." Anne said with a catch in her voice.

"Please, will you not call me "Abuelita," as Ramón does? It would give me great pleasure."

Trying to smile, Anne said, "Thank you—Abuelita. You have been so kind to me, I don't know how I am going to be able to go."

"Let us think no more about it," she said firmly. "You have seen the gown I bought for you to wear tonight? Good. How do you like it?"

Grateful, Anne followed Doña Isabel's lead, and, in her remorse that she had been so preoccupied she had not thought to express her pleasure and appreciation for the new dress, she found composure.

Staring at the dress some time later, Anne was still no closer to a decision on how she was going to break her mock engagement. Doña Isabel, when they had dis-

cussed the subject in those first days, had suggested a
public quarrel. It had not sounded difficult at the time,
perhaps because she was sure she would have Ramón's
support and cooperation. Now she was not so certain.

Doña Isabel's choice for something suitable in which
to celebrate the engagement was a floor-length gown of
palest blush pink. Lined with a stiff skirt of taffeta, the
laced-edged silk organza was, without subtlety, reminiscent of a wedding gown. It had been freshly pressed
and left hanging on a padded hanger under a protec-
tive covering of plastic.

It was lovely, the very thing to give, a delicate, ethe-
real look to a prospective bride; still, Anne could con-
jure up no excitement over wearing it. If things had
been different . . . No, she must not dwell on such
thoughts. She had enough to worry about without tor-
turing herself with what might have been.

She spent a long time in the bath, soaking in
scented water frothy with bath salts. It should have
been relaxing. It wasn't. As she lay with closed eyes,
she cudgeled her brain, trying to think of something,
anything, to use as an excuse to start a quarrel with
Ramón. What made men angry? Jealousy? Flirting
with other men? That might work, though more because of the affront to his pride than because of any
possessive instinct. The only trouble was that she was
not sure she could bring herself to do it in this country
where she was not acquainted with any other men.

It was possible that she could make a scene because
of his attentions to some other woman, except that
would be a tacit admission that she cared enough to be
jealous. She must avoid that at all costs.

At some point in the evening she could remove his
ring, place it in his hand, and walk away. However,
that was too obvious and public a rejection for her to
feel comfortable with it.

What was left? Snapping at him? Finding fault?

Being rude to his friends? Such tactics were so foreign to her personality she doubted her ability to carry them through.

She had to do something. She couldn't just drift along, waiting for Ramón to dismiss her, becoming more deeply involved, more vulnerable to his love making, each day. She had to cut herself loose, return to her plain, safe, ordinary life before it was too late. In time, this two weeks in Mexico would seem like a dream. The memories would fade. She would think of them less and less often, until eventually they would be forgotten. She would forget, she vowed, if it took the rest of her life.

Standing before the dressing table mirror, Anne took extra care with her makeup. Despite her intention of leaving, it seemed important that she look her best. She told herself it was for her own sake, for moral support; she would not admit that she wanted to make certain Ramón remembered her looking as attractive as possible.

Her eyes appeared enormous with mysterious shadowed depths, in the pale cameo of her face. Mascara, sparingly applied, served only to heighten the impression. Pink lip gloss was an improvement, as was a whisk of blusher on the cheekbones, but eye liner and shadow stood out so against her pallor that they had to be removed and the entire operation done over again.

Putting on makeup took longer than she expected. It was getting late when she turned finally to her hair. Thankfully, it was cooperative. Doña Isabel had offered to take Anne to her hairdresser again, but she had refused. She had shampooed her hair earlier in the day and set it in her usual manner. Now it hung in a smooth, silken bell which rested lightly on the top of her shoulders.

At last she was ready to put on the gown. As she took it from its hanger, she could not help remember-

ing the last time she had dressed for a formal evening
with Ramón. It had begun disastrously, with the
poblana dress, and ended much the same way. She
would never forget the combination of rage and pain
on Ramón's face when he had looked up and seen her
descending the stairs.

Yes she would. She must, for her own peace of
mind. And suddenly she knew how she would break
her engagement. She wanted to quarrel with him,
didn't she? She wanted to make a clean break, one
that would enable her to leave without regret. Well,
then, why not wear the *poblana* costume again? He
could not fail to be enraged, especially since he must
realize she knew the significance of it. If she dared
wear it, there was little doubt that she would be freed
at once of this masquerade. If she dared . . .

The costume with its skirt and blouse, its lace-edged
underskirt, vest, and fringed sash, had been picked up
by Carmelita and hung carefully away in the wardrobe.

With hands that trembled a little, Anne took it out.
Quickly, before she could change her mind, she put it
on, jerking the sash tight about her waist. With its
rich materials and intricate embroidery detailing, it was
still a handsome ensemble and Anne could not see that
it was markedly different from the peasant costumes,
the African- and Russian-derived gowns, which were
being worn for evening in the United States. With a
shake of her head, she turned from the mirror to look
for the low-heeled slippers which had come with it.

She could find only one. While she knelt with her
head in the wardrobe she thought she heard the sound
of a car on the drive. The noise sent a shiver of dread
along her spine, and she began to search frantically for
the missing slipper, piling the empty dress boxes and
tissue paper which littered the bottom of the wardrobe
out onto the floor.

When a knock came on the door she sat back on her

heels in relief. "Come in," she called, expecting to see the bright round face of Carmelita around the door.

She was mistaken. It was Ramón who pushed the panel wide and stepped into the room.

"Are you ready?" he asked. "The guests are arriving and we will be expected to greet them together."

The last few words of his sentence were delivered mechanically. He stopped in the doorway, all expression leaving his face as he stared at Anne kneeling in a billow of skirts before the wardrobe.

"I—thought you were Carmelita," Anne stammered, irritated at the same time with herself for the agitation which swept over her.

"I never imagined you expected me," he answered deliberately.

"I will be with you as—as soon as I find the other shoe."

"Don't trouble yourself," he said without raising his voice. "You are not going to need it."

The memory of the threat he had made before to take the dress off of her hung unspoken between them. Anne felt her heart accelerate at the grim look about his mouth. It may have been a trick of the light, but a tormented expression seemed to darken his eyes for an instant.

"Ramón . . ." Anne breathed in unconscious entreaty. A sense of guilt stabbed at her, as if she had purposely set out to hurt him. This was going all wrong. There should have been an audience to witness this meeting, to overhear the inevitable argument and realize the stalemate between them.

"Why?" he asked, pushing the door to and advancing into the room with dangerous feline grace. "Why tonight, of all nights?"

"I thought—that is, this is the last day of my two weeks. There must be an argument, a reason for breaking the engagement."

"I see," he said, averting his eyes as he gave a thoughtful nod.

"I have to go home," Anne said, a shade of desperation creeping into her voice. "I can't stay here."

"Can't you?" he queried, his voice soft, almost tentative.

He had said he wanted her, no more than that. He had never mentioned love. If she succumbed to a few kisses and an appeal to the senses, she would regret it for the rest of her life. What she felt had no place in a casual affair. To leave now would be difficult enough; later it might be more than she could bear.

"No," she replied unsteadily, "I can't."

In the quiet they heard the sound of another car on the drive below. Ramón stood totally still while seconds ticked past. Abruptly he raised his head.

"There will be no need for a disagreement. Our engagement can be ended easily enough without a public parting. We will not upset Abuelita by disrupting her party or putting a sudden end to her hopes. Later, when we have more time, we can discuss your departure."

"Very well," Anne answered, her voice so low it was barely audible to her own ears.

He flicked a glance at the pink gown she had left uncovered on its hanger. "For the moment, we are needed below. I will wait outside while you change. Five minutes, no more."

She emerged from the bedroom well within the deadline. Ramón was leaning on the opposite wall, his arms folded and a distant look on his face. He smiled when he saw her, a movement of the lips as brief and impersonal as the appraisal he gave her appearance. Without comment, he pushed erect with his shoulders, moving to her side, as she started along the hall. It was just as well he did not speak. So tightly knotted were the cords of her throat that she was not at all sure she could have managed an answer.

With his hand under her elbow, they descended the stairs. Anne was almost painfully aware of him as he moved beside her. She would not look directly at him, but as they passed a framed painting she caught a glimpse of him on the reflective surface of the glass, a tall distinguished man in correct evening attire. The pleated front of his shirt was immaculately white against the sun-burned darkness of his skin. In his lapel was a flower, something she had not noticed until this moment. Slanting a quick look at it, she saw it was a blush pink rosebud, the same color as her gown. For an instant she was puzzled, until she recognized the hand of his grandmother in the perfect match.

There was to be a small dinner party, consisting of Estela and Esteban, Señor and Señora Martínez, and a few more of Ramón's close business associates, before the larger entertainment began. As Anne and Ramón reached the hall, they could hear voices coming from the *sala* where the dinner guests were gathered. Over the babbling murmur one female voice rose loud and clear. Hearing it, Anne came to a halt. It was Irene. The woman had to have invited herself for Anne knew her name had not been on the list of dinner guests, though she was included for later.

"Courage, Anne," Ramón said, tilting his head so he could look into her pale set face. "It is only a party."

"I know," she replied, trying to smile. "But Irene— we weren't expecting her. The table arrangements . . ."

"The table arrangements are no longer your concern. Let María and the servants worry about it. You have nothing to do except take what enjoyment you can from the evening."

"But your cousin . . ."

"She cannot hurt you." A speculative gleam warmed his narrowed eyes. "You have nothing to fear from her this night. Only once have I seen you more beautiful than you are now, and then because the nightgown you wore was somewhat more—revealing. You remember? It was the same color as this dress my scheming grandmother has chosen for you."

Anne threw a startled look at him as the wild rose color of confusion spread across her cheekbones. Of course she remembered. That first night, the nightgown the housekeeper, María, had found for her, the pain in her head, the embarrassing confrontation in the hall when she had ventured out to find relief. It was not every day that a man swept her into his arms and carried her to her bed. How could she forget? What was astonishing was that he remembered such a detail as the color of her nightgown.

"That's better," he said, a low note of laughter in his voice as he placed his arm around her, urging her gently toward the sala. "At least now you no longer look as if you were going to your doom."

The purpose of the compliment was obvious, still Anne could not help but be affected by it. She felt attractive as she moved into the room, able to greet the guests and accept their congratulations with smiling ease. Even Irene posed no threat to her composure, though the other woman immediately capped her best wishes by introducing the man at her side as her fiancé.

It was the same Mexican with whom Anne had danced two nights before. Though his full name eluded her, she discovered that he was called Pépé. He seemed a little discomfited at Irene's public proclamation of their relationship and her possessive clinging. Of slight build, he wore his fine dark hair brushed straight back. Despite the stamp of Spanish pride on his features, Anne doubted he was a match for the woman at his side. The whispered remonstrance he made when Anne and Ramón turned away received no more than a laugh from Irene.

The dinner went smoothly. The food was delicious, the service perfect, leaving little excuse for Anne to allow her attention to wander from the general conversation.

Doña Isabel, installed at the foot of the table with Esteban on one hand and an elderly gentleman, Señor Rivas, on the other, was in high form. She fairly sparkled with good humor, chiding her grandson for his silence and skillfully drawing each of the other diners out. In a most genteel way she even flirted a bit with Señor Rivas, who gallantly responded in kind. When Doña Isabel had added his name to the seating plan, she had said something offhand about evening the numbers, but Anne suspected the older woman enjoyed his company more than she admitted.

Places had been found for Irene and her new fiancé at the table. Irene was seated next to Señor Rivas, with Señor Martínez and Estela beyond her on Ramón's left. Pépé was between Anne, at the place of honor on Ramón's right hand, and Señora Martínez, with Esteban beyond the señora on Doña Isabel's left. That the arrangement was none too pleasing to Irene was plain, though her reasons had more to do with her distance from the head of the table than with her separation from her fiancé. Several times she leaned forward with a question designed to capture Ramón's interest. Without effort, Doña Isabel foiled these attempts, doing it so sweetly that Irene could not take offense without appearing boorish.

Her antics were not lost on Pépé. Irene's fiancé watched her with sullen suspicion in his face. When she flung him no more than a perfunctory smile, he grew steadily more morose, draining his wine glass again and again as the meal progressed.

If Ramón caught this byplay, he gave no sign. He,

too, as Doña Isabel had remarked, seemed more preoccupied than usual. For a brief instant Anne allowed
herself to think that her refusal to stay had meant
more to him then she supposed. That thought was
quickly ousted by the dread that it was Irene's announcement which had disturbed him.

Did he, in spite of everything, feel some attachment
for Irene? Suppose he had merely been using the silly
little American girl who had forced herself upon him
to teach his countrywoman not to take him for granted?
Or worse still, suppose he was using Anne to distract
Doña Isabel's attention from the woman to whom his
grandmother had taken a dislike?

Such thoughts were bitter company. Though she
tried, Anne could not quite dislodge them from her
mind.

Staring at the candle flames which wavered in a low
silver holder nestled in a bed of yellow dahlias, Anne
thought it was just as well she would soon be leaving.
If she had to stay and endure the torture of such
doubts for long, she would go mad.

Beside her, Pépé, perhaps deciding to take a page
from his fiancée's book, inclined his head in Anne's
direction with a low-voiced comment. She hardly
heard, so deep was her concentration.

She glanced once more at Ramón to find his considering gaze riveted upon her face. Twin flames, the
reflection of the candles, burned in his eyes. For an instant she was aware of a sudden breathless warmth in
the room, then she realized his stare had moved past
her to the man at her side. Sick at heart, she recognized the emotion which flared white-hot in his steady
regard. It was jealousy.

They were just leaving the dining room when the
guests invited later for the dance began to arrive.
Laughing, talking, accepting glasses of champagne
from deferential waiters, they crowded into the sala.

They were a glittering throng with one thing in common, an air of expectancy.

It was Doña Isabel, standing regal in her lavender lace, who made the formal announcement of the engagement. The words, in liquid, sonorous Spanish, had a misleading finality to Anne's ears. Side by side, she and Ramón accepted the first toast. They sipped once at their champagne glasses, then at the instigation of the elderly woman, linked arms to drink again.

With the eyes of everyone in the room upon them, Ramón stood smiling down at her. The contours of his mouth curved in an expression so loving that Anne had to clench her teeth to keep her own smile from wobbling. Deliberately, he took her free hand, and holding her gaze with his own, raised it, uncurling the fingers. He pressed his mouth, warm and firm, to the softness of her palm.

Anne caught her breath. She would have snatched her hand away if he had not held it fast. A moment later, the orchestra hired for the occasion struck up the first ceremonial waltz. Placing her captured hand on his shoulder, Ramón swept her out onto the floor which had been cleared for dancing.

They danced without speaking, circling the floor alone once before they were joined by other couples. Anne, becoming aware after a moment of the mechanical stiffness of her performance, made an effort to pull herself together. She was not helped by the steely feel of the arms which held her close against him.

"I believe it's time I congratulated you on your acting ability," she said, flicking an upward glance through her lashes.

He accepted the compliment calmly. "There's no telling what heights we might reach, you and I, with a little more practice."

Was there an oblique suggestion in his tone? Anne drew back in his arms. "You promised . . ."

"Did I?"

"You said we would discuss my leaving later on."

"So I did," he agreed, his voice hardening. "I wonder what is behind your persistence in bringing this subject up every time we are together. What is your hurry to get back to Texas? What are you running away from—or who are you running to?"

Anne felt her heart jerk. It was an effort to hold her voice steady. "There's nothing like that. I just want to go back where I belong, back to being plain ordinary Anne Matthews. Is that so hard to understand?"

"No," he answered. "Not if it is the truth."

"You doubt my word?" A small frown drew her brows together.

"Let us just say I have little hope of a straight answer from you."

Anne came to a halt, making a futile effort to free herself of his arms. They were near the edge of the dance floor. His hands cupping her elbows, Ramón shielded her from view with his broad back.

"You are angry?" he asked. "Very well. Shall we put it to the test? Tell me this. Are you running away from me?"

Anne went still, her eyes wide as she searched the stiff angles of his face. How was she to reply? A negative answer would be a lie. She was running away from him, trying to escape the effect he had on her senses and the disruption he had caused in her life. And if she answered yes, he would believe she was afraid of him, fearful that he might press his attentions upon her. Neither of those things were true.

And yet, her silence was in itself an answer.

After a moment he dropped his hands and stepped back. His eyelids narrowed, shuttering his eyes, but not before she saw the derision mirrored in their black surface.

"Ramón . . ." she said, touching his coat sleeve with cool fingers. "You don't understand."

His smile was bleak as he inclined his head. "Are you certain you do?" he asked, and turning on his heel as the music came to an end, he walked away.

Anne did not have time to determine the meaning of his cryptic remark. She was claimed immediately for a bossa-nova by Pépé, who seemed delighted to teach her the unfamiliar steps. Afterward she danced a stately measure, with Señor Rivas, followed in turn by Señor Martínez, and still Ramón did not come near her again. He led his grandmother out onto the floor, then stood beside her chair, leaving her only to solicit what were clearly duty dances with Señora Martínez and one or two other elderly women and young female relatives. Soon afterward, he disappeared, remaining away for nearly an hour. During that interval Anne noticed Irene leaving the room, however, she did not stay away for any length of time.

The relief Anne felt at seeing her return alone and with a frown of discontent marring her features was so intense that she sought a chair against the wall beside Doña Isabel. She remained there for fully half an hour.

The musicians which had been hired for the occasion were adept at modern music as well as the traditional Latin rhythms. It was interesting to watch young Mexicans in expensive evening wear gyrating to sounds she associated in her mind with American teenagers in blue jeans and T-shirts. They were an attractive people, Anne found herself thinking. With a more discerning eye than she had had when she arrived two weeks before, she could trace, in their high cheekbones and brilliant, flashing eyes, indications of their Aztec lineage. She could not begin to remember all their names, though most had been painstakingly introduced by Doña Isabel. Still, when they caught her eyes, these friends and distant relatives of Ramón gave her spontaneous smiles of acceptance that warmed her even though she knew she would never be one of them.

It was Pépé, his invitation a model of decorum, who succeeded in prying her from Doña Isabel's side. He was helped considerably by the reappearance of Ramón. As Anne caught sight of him making his way toward them around the dance floor, she knew a moment of unreasoning panic which drove her out onto the floor.

It was when Irene's fiancé took her in his arms that Anne discovered why he was so careful in his speech, so studied in his movements. He was somewhat the worse for drink. His tongue had a tendency to betray him by slurring his consonants if he spoke too quickly. Though he had not reached the point where he was unsteady on his feet, he was close to it. His breath smelled strongly of alcohol. He had also the delusion of the intoxicated about his singing ability, for he insisted on crooning the words to the music into Anne's ear.

"Are you certain you want to dance?" Anne asked with a shade of annoyance as he stepped on her toes for the third time.

"Thousand apologies," he murmured. "Si, si, I must dance. My Irene told me to go away and amuse myself, and I like to dance with pretty Americans."

"I appreciate the compliment, but I don't think you are in any shape to dance with anyone," Anne told him.

The drinks that were being circulated by the waiters were not, she knew, strong enough to account for Pépé's condition. She strongly suspected him of carrying his own flask or having access to a supply in his automobile outside.

He drew himself up as straight as he was able. "Are you saying I may be drunk?" he inquired.

"That is exactly what I am saying," Anne assured him.

He considered that. "You may be right," he said with a wise nod.

With the press of people in the room, the French doors which lined one side of the *sala* had been thrown open. Through these stole the faint ghost of a breeze to fan Anne's heated cheeks.

Drawing a deep breath, Anne said pointedly, "Don't you think we should sit down then?"

"To sit idle and watch my Irene dancing with Señor Castillo?" he asked, tilting his head to the area of the floor where Irene was just moving into Ramón's arms. "No, that is too much the tame dog. I will not. I will go outside, that is what I will do. Outside, where the air is fresh." A grin, half-foolish, half-pained, curled around his thin lips. "Will you step out with me into the patio?"

His suggestion seemed suddenly reasonable to Anne. She, too, could use a breath of untainted air. In addition, she felt sorry for Irene's fiancé. His position—being used as a handy face-saver for the Mexican woman—was not an enviable one. If he cared at all for her, there was some excuse for his over-indulgence.

"All right," she agreed wearily, "but only for a moment.

After the smoke-filled, over-heated closeness of the *sala*, the cool air of the patio was like mountain-cooled wine. Anne needed no urging to stroll along the arcade, away from the loud music and the confusion of voices. She even found herself grateful to Pépé for his suggestion. Getting away from the responsibility of being the guest of honor, constantly on view, was an unexpected relief.

"Señorita Matthews?" Pépé said, ambling to a halt.

"Yes?" Anne replied.

"You—like me, señorita?"

"What do you mean?" Anne asked, made wary by something she could not identify in his manner.

"As a man!" he exclaimed, his expression in the dim light from the curtain windows plainly showing that he found her dense.

"How can you expect me to answer that," Anne edged, "When you know I am engaged to Ramón?"

"I did not expect you to come outside with me because you are the *novia* of Ramón, and yet, here you are."

"Oh? I had not realized it was—indiscreet. I suspect we had better go back inside," Anne said, swinging around.

"No, no," he said, reaching out to catch her arm. "I did not mean to make you angry. I only—I only wanted an answer to my question. Irene has said to me that I am lucky she wishes to make herself my wife. She says I am not the kind of man who is attractive to many women."

Her attention caught, Anne turned back. "Surely you must have met many young women who were—who responded to the compliments you paid them?"

"Yes, but perhaps they were only pretending," he said in a quiet tone, a scowl crumbling his face as though he was trying to keep from crying.

If he had been sober, Anne thought swiftly, he would have died before saying such a thing aloud. She did not need to ask if Irene had planted that doubt also. Why would she say such cruel things? What kind of person was she to want him to follow like a tame dog at her heels, grateful for the bones of affection she might throw him? What a terrible ego she must have.

On impulse she covered Pépé fingers with her own where they clutched at her arm. "Pay no heed to Irene, Pépé. There are many women who could love you."

"Ah, señorita," he said, his voice husky, "I knew you were kind . . . and generous—"

With a quickness and rawhide strength belied by his appearance, he pulled her into his arms. Surprise held her immobile while his lips slid across her cheek to her mouth. An instant later, she broke his grip, stepping back to arm's length.

"You . . ." she began, fumbling for words in her incoherent anger.

She never completed the sentence.

"Well, Ramón?" Irene, her voice dripping satisfaction like honey, spoke from the open French window. "It looks as though we have both been made to look like fools."

Pépé recovered first, starting forward. "Irene, my love, my heart, let me explain."

"Explain?" she jeered. "Pray tell me how? Are you going to ask me to doubt the evidence of my own eyes?"

She stepped out into the shadowed arcade, leaving a clear view of Ramón just behind her with Doña Isabel at his side. The sight of his host seemed to throw Pépé's befuddled mind into greater confusion, and he made an abortive movement as though he would protect Anne from Ramón's wrath.

The gesture enraged Irene. "No doubt you mean to give yourself time to think up a plausible lie? You can save yourself the trouble. Neither Ramón nor I will be stupid enough to believe you. Will we, my dear Ramón?"

Feeling as though she was caught in a nightmare, Anne turned toward the man in the doorway. Surely he would put a stop to Irene's relentless browbeating of the young man.

The contempt that blazed in his eyes as they raked over her came as a complete shock. She was too numb to wonder at the whiteness about his compressed lips or the pulsating nerve that rippled the skin of his clenched jaw.

"No, I doubt my opinion of my fiancée." he grated, emphasizing the last word, "can be altered—for better or worse."

Doña Isabel glanced from Anne's pale, frozen features to her grandson. "My dear Ramón," she said in a frail voice. "Things may not be as bad as they seem."

"No," he said, "they are probably worse."

His words, for all their quietness, cut into Anne like the lash of a whip. In the reflex of pain, she struck back.

"Never mind, Abuelita," she said, her voice trembling. "Trust is too much to expect of Don Ramón Carlos Castillo."

Her words seemed to snap the iron restraint which held him. He strode forward, his fingers biting into her arms as he dragged her from Pépé's side. She fell against his chest and he pushed her upright, giving her a hard shake.

"Trust is something you earn," he ground out, his eyes boring into hers. "It is given as a reward to those who have proven themselves worthy of it. You, my dear Anne, my beautiful cheat, have not!"

Anne, shivering with fury and a primitive reaction to his violence that she refused to recognize, opened her mouth. But he would not let her speak.

"I was beginning to believe your innocent pose, beginning to believe you had told the truth from the first. No more..."

He got no further. Irene's piercing shriek cut across his words, a gasping sound that went on and on.

With a shaking finger she pointed to Doña Isabel like a crumpled doll on the flagstones. Her face was the color of chalk and her breathing shallow and fast as Anne stumbled to her knees beside the still figure. Picking up her hand, she found the small, bony fingers as cold as ice.

Ramón, dropping to a crouch on the other side of

his grandmother, felt for her pulse. Flicking a hard look up at Irene, he snapped, "Stop that noise! Call the doctor—Abuelita's personal physician, not your own choice."

With a tenderness at variance with the harsh frown on his face, he straightened Doña Isabel's limbs, then gently lifted her in his arms. "Go ahead and make her bed ready," he said to Anne, his voice devoid of anything other than concern for his grandmother.

Irene had stopped shrieking, but she seemed unable to move. Pépé shot a hesitant glance at her, then swallowed convulsively, putting his shoulders back. "Which doctor?" he asked.

Ramón told him. Nodding to Anne, he said, "The curtains." When she sprang to hold them back, he carried Doña Isabel through into the sala.

A crowd had begun to gather in that end of the room. Ramón pushed through without ceremony, leaving Anne to explain the collapse as best she could.

It was Estela who provided the most acceptable explanation. Her wide eyes filling with tears, she murmured, "Poor Abuelita. The excitement must have been too much for her."

Ramón did not appear to be moving fast, yet he had reached Doña Isabel's bedroom before Anne caught up with him. Patiently he waited while Anne pushed open the door, then ran to throw back the covers.

He placed his burden on the bed with care, then straightened, standing once more with his fingers on her pulse.

Anne moved to the other side of the bed. She thought there was a little more color to the pale cheeks, a less pinched look about the mouth. The elderly woman's breathing had slowed to a regular rhythm. Under Anne's fingers her pulse felt a trifle fast, but strong.

Anne raised her eyes to the man on the other side of

the bed. He did not notice. The skin tight across his cheekbones with strain, he stared down at his grandmother as if willing her to live.

The door of the bedroom swung noiselessly open as Estela, followed closely by the housekeeper, María, entered. "The doctor is on his way," Ramón's sister said in a low voice. "Most of the guests are leaving, except for a few who are waiting for news. Is she . . . she's not . . ."

"She is still unconscious," Ramón said in a clipped tone.

"Your pardon, Don Ramón," María murmured. "If you will permit . . ." Politely, but firmly María took Ramón's place beside the bed.

"Perhaps we should undress her," Estela said unhappily. "She would be more comfortable."

"Loosen her clothing, by all means," Ramón said, "but disturb her as little as possible until the doctor arrives."

María nodded. "I will manage," she said, and waited expectantly for them to leave the room while she performed this task. There seemed little reason not to comply for the moment.

On the far side of the bed, Anne was one of the last to leave the room. As she looked back she thought she saw Doña Isabel's eyelids flutter, opening to a slit. A moment later María, her face impassive, stepped into Anne's line of vision, interposing herself between the door and the figure in the bed.

They had still not been readmitted to the bedroom when the doctor arrived. His examination, conducted with only María present, was a lengthy one.

Emerging from the room at last, he turned to face the relatives and friends gathered in the hall. His face solemn, he gave a courteous nod of recognition to Anne and Estela, but it was to Ramón that he addressed his remarks.

"Your grandmother has had a traumatic shock combined with a fall, never a minor matter for one her age. As you know, her health has not been robust for some years, and I feel that the wisest course, at this time, is to ensure that she has complete bed rest plus total tranquility. She must not be disturbed or upset in any way. How seriously ill she is remains to be seen. For the present, I have given her a sedative which should allow her to sleep for some hours. When she awakens you may find a marked improvement, then again, you may not. I recommend a close watch upon her for the next, say, twenty-four hours, though with a mimimun of visitors. There should be only one person with her at any given time. The most important thing is to see that she remains quiet." A few more instructions, another nod, and the interview was over.

María could not be dissuaded from taking the first watch. Because of their children at home, Estela and Esteban could not stay, but Estela promised to sit with Doña Isabel during the afternoon if Ramón and Anne could manage until then.

Estela, distressed that she would not be able to contribute more to her grandmother's care, suggested hiring a private nurse. Ramón vetoed the idea, at least until after the doctor's stipulated twenty-four-hour period had passed. On that grave note they parted.

Chapter 10

Anne spent the remaining hours of the night tossing fitfully on her bed. She could not calm herself enough to sleep. Each time she tried, Ramón's accusing eyes burned into her brain and she felt herself caught once more in the merciless grip of his rage. She told herself she hated him for daring to suspect her of such shameful behavior and for the terrible things he had said to her—that she didn't care if she never saw him again. She called herself a fool for letting him disturb her rest. She lashed herself for being unfeeling because her thoughts kept turning to her confrontation with him instead of to the health of his grandmother.

One moment she occupied her mind by thinking of the devastating things she could have said to him to make him sorry he had doubted her. The next, she found herself making excuses for his actions, placing the blame on Irene, on his mother, who had made him cynical about women, on his upbringing, the society in which he lived, anything and anywhere, except where it belonged.

He was proud and arrogant, hard, unreasonable, and tempermental, she told herself—and remembered instead the sweet tenderness of the kisses he had given her and the gentle touch of his hands upon an unconscious old woman.

Toward dawn she dozed for an hour or so, though

the snatched moments of sleep could not have been called restful. When she opened her eyes, the pale yellow light of the early morning sun was filtering into the room. Feeling heavy-limbed and drugged with weariness, Anne slid out of bed. She splashed water over her face in an attempt to feel more alert, then slipped into her clothes and ran a comb through her hair.

There were purple shadows under her eyes and the smooth skin stretched over her cheekbones was colorless, but with a tiny shrug, she turned away from the mirror. What did it matter how she looked? There was no one who would notice, or care.

Her footsteps made no sound on the thick oriental rug as she moved along the hall. Pausing outside the door fo Doña Isabel's room, she rapped softly on the panel with her knuckles, then swung it open.

It was dark inside, the only light coming from the window, where a single panel of the heavy draperies had been pulled aside. As she entered, a shadowy figure rose from a chair placed near the light, a figure too tall, even in the dimness, to be María.

Anne stopped. "I didn't know you had relieved María," she said, stiffening as she recognized Ramón. "I'll come back later."

She was already turning away when his voice reached her. "No," he said. "Abuelita was awake a short time ago. She asked for you."

"For me?"

Ramón ran his hand over his head to the back of his neck in a harassed gesture. "She insisted on seeing you as early as possible this morning. She—I believe she has something she wants to say to you. It will be better, perhaps, if she gets it off her mind. Would you wait here until she wakes again?"

"Of course," Anne agreed. Though she could not be sure, she thought Ramón hesitated a moment as though there was something he would add.

"Yes?" she asked half expecting him to give her some caution or instruction, or make a suggestion concerning his grandmother's comfort.

"It was nothing," he said brusquely. Stepping past her, he left the room, closing the door with a gentle click.

Frowning, Anne moved across to the chair Ramón had vacated. As she sank down into it, she found that it was still warm from his body. She leaned back, closing her eyes for an instant.

Very soon she must get away from this place, though how she was to broach the subject again to Ramón in his present mood she could not imagine. Taking a deep breath, she let it out in a long sigh. Perhaps it was just as well that he was angry with her. If she could find a way to bring the matter to his attention once more, he should be as anxious as she was to see that particular request granted.

From the direction of the bed came the rustle of bedcovers. Instantly alert, Anne jumped up, moving toward the bed.

"Turn on the light, child," Doña Isabel said, her voice surprisingly strong. "I am not asleep."

Anne changed directions, going to the wall switch. As light sprang brightly into every corner of the room, she saw the elderly woman pushing herself up to a sitting position in the bed. Swiftly Anne moved to help her prop against several pillows.

"Don't fuss, dear, I'm not an invalid yet," Doña Isabel scolded before patting the edge of the bed. "Here, sit down beside me where I can see you and we can talk without disturbing anyone."

"Should you be sitting up?" Anne asked, a shade of anxiety in her tone as she complied. "I would never be able to forgive myself if I let you do more than you should."

Settling back, Doña Isabel folded her hands over the

sheet across her lap. "I am perfectly capable of deciding what I feel like doing."

Anne braved the trace of hauteur in the old woman's manner. "The doctor left orders that you were to have rest and quiet for twenty-four hours."

"Impossible," Doña Isabel declared.

"Perhaps another sedative?" Anne suggested, her gold-flecked eyes level as she watched the effect.

"I won't take it because, as you may have guessed, dear Anne, I don't need it."

The suspicion Anne had not allowed herself to consider was a fact then. Intuitively she had known it, and yet the doctor's grave attitude and strict instructions had caused her to doubt her instinct. Before she could speak, she had to be absolutely certain, however.

"What do you mean?" she asked.

Doña Isabel looked away with a grimace. "I thought you knew. Must I say it in plain English? All right, then. There was nothing wrong with me last night. There is nothing, beyond a few bruises, wrong with me now."

"Why?" Anne asked, the question coming out with a blunter sound than she had intended.

Doña Isabel turned back sharply. "You needn't make it sound as though I had committed a crime. I had to do something. What else could it be except faint? I twisted my knee as I fell, you know, and I'm not certain I didn't actually lose consciousness for a few minutes. I could not let my grandson mistrust you, nor could I let the two of you ruin your lives just because of Irene's spiteful jealousy. I saw you go out with that inebriated fool, Pépé. I saw Irene as she suggested to Ramón that they see what you were up to with her young man. It is difficult for one woman to fool another; I knew she would cause a scene if she could possibly manage it. I did not expect you, my child, to cooperate with her to the extent of allowing yourself to be found in Pépé's arms."

Anne started to protest, but the old lady waved her explanations away. "Never mind. It was plain enough what happened. But I could not bear to let it all end for such a silly, meaningless episode."

"It might have been better if you had," Anne said slowly. "It was you who suggested Ramón and I end this farce of an engagement with a public disagreement."

"I've had second thoughts since then." A triumphant gleam appeared in Doña Isabel's eyes. "Tell me," she continued, "what is the most common way to end an engagement?"

"If not by a quarrel, then I guess by the common consent of both parties," Anne answered reasonably.

"No. no. Don't be dense, my dear. The most common way of ending one is by marriage."

Anne stared at her. Slowly she got to her feet. "What are you suggesting?"

"Why, that you wed my grandson with the blessing of God, the church, and myself . . ."

"You seem to have forgotten that your grandson despises me, that he has never had the least desire to marry me," Anne said through stiff lips.

"That isn't true," Doña Isabel said with confidence. "I have put the proposal before Ramón, and he has agreed."

"You . . . you suggested this marriage to Ramón?"

"I did. He made no objections. Indeed, he was most anxious . . ."

Anne cut across her words without apology. "Are you sure he made no objections because he had none, or because he was afraid to upset you just now?"

"Does it matter," the old woman asked, her voice curiously gently. "So long as he has given his word that he will make you his wife?"

"Yes. Yes, it does. He doesn't love me."

"But you love him, my proud lucifer of a grandson—do you not?" Doña Isabel asked, and sat quietly waiting for Anne's reply.

After a long moment, Anne nodded.

"Isn't that enough for now? That, and the chance to win his love in time?"

"No," Anne said, her voice shaking. "No, it isn't. I don't want a man who doesn't care for me, one who has to be forced to the altar."

"But Anne," she protested, "reconsider, please. It is all arranged."

"Then you must tell him that I will not hold him to the bargain."

"Do not be hasty. Think it over for a day or two at least," Doña Isabel pleaded.

"I—I can't," Anne answered, trying to smile. She did not want such a temptation dangling before her for so long. She was far too uncertain of her power to resist it.

A frown of concern drew the older woman's fine gray brows together. "Anne, please, for my sake," she said holding out her hand.

Anne took it with fingers that trembled a little. "You must not ask it of me," she said in a voice husky with tears. "I feel honored that you went to such trouble for me, and I am grateful, but this is something I cannot do."

On impulse she leaned forward and pressed her lips to the soft crepe skin of Doña Isabel's cheek. The old lady squeezed her hand, then let it go. "Well, then," she said, smiling a little, then lifting her chin. "You must do as you think best. There is one problem you cannot have considered, however."

After a quick review, Anne asked, "What is it?"

"I can trust you, I know, not to give me away to Ramón. How are you going to explain not complying with what might have been my deathbed wish in this matter without making yourself appear hard of heart?"

"I thought you . . ."

"I?"

"You could tell him I was reluctant. Surely that would be enough?"

"Enough to make him feel obligated to use his own methods of persuasion." She tilted her head. "No, I thought you would not like that."

"Doña Isabel . . ." Anne began, desperation shading her voice.

"I don't wish to seem unkind, but I cannot help you in this, even if I wanted to. You owe Ramón an explanation for your refusal, don't you think?"

"Perhaps I might, if he had asked me, but not in a case like this. Anyway, he knows how I feel."

"Does he? Does he know exactly how you feel—about him?"

Under the old lady's piercing eye, Anne could only shake her head.

Doña Isabel relaxed against her pillows. "I thought not. Sometimes I have wondered—but never mind. The only thing I can suggest, my dear, is to wait. Perhaps in a week or so I will be able to throw off this invalid's pose and you will be able to discuss the possibility of this marriage with Ramón without pressure."

The thought made Anne feel sick with dread but she saw nothing to be gained from arguing further. She agreed.

"In the meantime," Doña Isabel said with a tight smile, "I suppose I must play my part a little longer. If you will, please ring for María. I feel the need, just now, of my morning chocolate, and then a hot bath."

For the sake of appearances Anne waited until María came before slipping away. The old lady, basking under the torrent of scolding Spanish, did not notice her leave.

Back in her room, she moved to the window and stood staring out. A merciful numbness gripped her. Her mind held room for a single thought. She had made her choice; there was no going back.

It was the right decision, she knew that. Still, it would not be an easy decision to hold to if she had to face Ramón again. She knew herself to be vulnerable to his persuasion. Hadn't she yielded to it once before by staying in Mexico? No, she could not trust herself not to be swayed by his unrelenting logic.

Worse still was the thought of seeing him play the concerned and dutiful grandson, offering a suit to a woman he must despise.

It was safer, far safer, not to see him, to remember him as the angry, abusive man who had dug his fingers into her arms last night.

If she could do that, if she could remember him that way, then she might be able to exist long enough to forget the other times—times when they had laughed together, when he had held her in his arms and taken her lips in sweet, loveless passion.

Blindly, she turned from the window. Her handbag lay on the dressing table. Inside it was the money from the check Iva had sent her, her emergency fund. After what had happened she could not ask Ramón to arrange her flight home. She could not risk the possibility of refusal if she failed to do as he wanted, or the methods he might use to ensure that she stayed. She would go now.

It should not be hard to make her escape. There had been a constant stream of people coming and going in the house for the past few days. Doubtless there would be more today as the caterers cleared away, and those who had heard of Doña Isabel's collapse came to inquire after her health. Certainly, with the elderly woman lying ill upstairs, the servants would have little concern for the movements of Don Ramón's fiancée. With a little ingenuity she should be able to make her escape.

She would have to travel light, but that was no hardship. There was very little that she wished to carry with her. She was wearing her own cream-colored suit and that was all she wanted. She did not feel as if any of the other expensive clothes hanging in the wardrobe belonged to her, nor did she need them to hang in her closet at home as unworn reminders.

The turquoise pendant had been a gift from Doña Isabel to Ramón's fiancée. Since she had been that in name only, it was not hers to keep. She lingered over the statuette of the Virgin of Guadaloupe. The worn, wooden features seemed to reproach her. No, she could not take the Virgin from Mexico, no matter the wrench it cost to leave her behind.

She had almost reached the door on her way out when she remembered her engagement ring. Without the weight of the oval-shaped diamond, her finger felt light and curiously naked. With fingers that trembled, she placed it in plain view on the dressing table beside the pendant. She walked away without looking back.

All her fears of being stopped before she could leave the house were for nothing. It could not have been easier. With her head high and her handbag clutched in her fingers, she walked down the stairs.

In the hallway she paused, wondering where Ramón was. Even as the thought crossed her mind, she heard his voice, mingling with that of his secretary, coming from the study.

Clenching her teeth, she continued along the hall and let herself out the front door. It closed softly, firmly, behind her.

A gardener was on duty at the front gate, She gave him a smile and a pleasant nod as she passed. The gate was closed this morning but not locked. She slipped through it without assistance and turned to face the long sidewalk stretching empty before her.

As she walked bells began to ring, the mellow, silver-toned bells of Mexico, signaling early Sunday morning Mass. Unconsciously she kept time to their doleful chime, allowing the sound to crowd thought from her mind.

She only had to wait a few minutes for a bus heading down-town. She was not choosy; she took the first that came along, stepping off it in the center of the business district.

With a set and purposeful face, she made her way to the nearest large tourist hotel. For a modest tip the doorman flagged a taxi for her and even directed the driver to the International Airport.

The interior of the cab was none too clean and the springs of the back seat were broken down, still Anne leaned back, closing her eyes.

She was satisfied that her actions should make it unlikely that anyone could direct Ramón after her.

No, making her escape had not been hard. In the end, it had been simplicity itself. The difficult part still lay ahead of her—returning home and trying to pretend that nothing had changed, knowing all the time that nothing would ever be the same.

Anne pushed through the glass doors of Metcalf's Caterers with her hands pushed into her pockets and her chin tucked into the collar of her heavy navy pea jacket. Sliding the strap of her shoulder bag off her shoulder, she slung it onto the rack in the corner.

Iva Metcalf, seated at the reception desk, looked up. An intent look in her eyes, she surveyed Anne without speaking. When at last she ventured a remark, her tone was noncommittal.

"Still cold out?"

"Freezing!" Anne said with a realistic shudder. "And getting colder by the minute. I wouldn't be surprised if we had snow by morning. The wind is enough to cut you to the bone, straight out of the North."

"You should have more padding to protect your bones," Iva told her with a rueful glance down at her own ample proportions.

Anne smiled, then reluctantly slid out of her jacket before passing into the humid warmth of the big kitchen. Within seconds Iva followed her.

"How about a cup of coffee?" she said. "You look like you could use it, and my nerves tell me it's time for my last transfusion of the day. Some lady forgot to pick up her husband's birthday cake, too. His loss is our gain. Want a piece?"

"No, thanks," Anne answered, though she accepted the cup Iva poured from the ever-simmering coffee machine.

Paying no attention, Iva cut two generous slices and placed them on plates. "Afraid of spoiling your dinner that is, if you intend to have any?" Anne's employer asked, plonking one of the plates down in front of her. "Eat it. We're going to have to fatten you up before the next northerner blows you away. You're skinny as a rail and getting thinner every day. Your eyes look like somebody drew them in with a charcoal pencil. You are going to have to slow down. You may be making a mint of money working overtime for Metcalf's, but you're a terrible advertisement for the food we serve."

Anne laughed, as she was supposed to, and she tried to eat the cake Iva had cut for her. After one or two bites she put down her fork and pushed the plate away.

Watching her, Iva said seriously, "I mean it, Anne. If you go on like this, you'll make yourself sick. I've tried not to interfere since you came back from Mexico, but these last two weeks I've watched you melt away in front of my eyes. You can't go on like this."

"I—suppose it will get better eventually," Anne said with a tremulous movement of the lips.

"Not unless you help yourself." Iva sipped her coffee then sat swirling the black liquid with an elaborately casual manner. It was quiet in the corner where they sat on stools drawn up to the pastry counter. The chef, Tony, muttered to himself as he stirred something that looked like a cream sauce on the enormous range at the far end of the room. Joe had gone to deliver an order of hors d'oeuvres for a cocktail party. They were virtually alone.

When Anne made no answer, Iva glanced at her from the corner of her eye. "You never said much about what happened between you and your Mexican millionaire, and I've tried to mind my own business. But when you came back from down there anyone could tell you had been knocked for a loop. You can tell me to keep out of it if you want to—and I wouldn't blame you if you did—but sometimes it helps to talk about these things." `

"There's really not much to tell," Anne said, helpless before the other woman's combination of curiosity, real concern, and something more, something Anne could not quite define.

"Of course, if you don't want to discuss it . . ." Iva said, withdrawing at once in the face of Anne's reluctance.

Suddenly, when it looked as if the opportunity to speak to someone of what had taken place in Mexico was going to be taken away, Anne wanted to talk about it. It might well be the only chance she would have to straighten things out in her own mind, to apportion blame and pain once and for all.

By the time she finished her tale the coffee cups had

been emptied, refilled, then emptied again and the dregs left to grow cold.

A frown that was just the least bit prejudiced between her eyes, Iva said, "Well, at least you proved to Ramón Castillo that you weren't after his money."

With a wan nod, Anne agreed. "For what consolation that may be to me."

"You sound almost as if you regret not taking them up on their offer," Iva commented, her gaze narrowing.

Catching her breath, Anne looked away. Did she? She could not tell. Sometimes it seemed that if she had been less proud, less determined to have everything or nothing, she might have found a measure of happiness. Often at night, lying alone in her bed, she had found herself yearning against all reason for the half a loaf that had been offered to her.

If there had ever been a time when she had nourished a secret hope that Ramón might follow her, it had been of short duration. She had had no communication whatever with the Castillo family.

She lived alone these days. Judy had moved out of the apartment. Fired by Anne's example, and what Judy thought of as her romantic adventure in a foreign land, she had persuaded her parents to let her go to Iran to work in the oil fields. By the time Anne returned, she was packing to leave. Denied the presence of her roommate, Anne had been thrown back on her own company, forced to live with her own image of what had occurred. It was a relief to have it out in the open, and yet it was disturbing to have her vain regrets put into words.

Oddly persistent, Iva's voice reached Anne in her absorption. "Do you regret leaving? Do you still feel anything for Ramón?"

"I wonder sometimes what would have happened if I had stayed," Anne admitted. "As for what I feel, I don't think I could ever love any other man."

Iva nodded, a frown pleating her forehead. Absent-mindly, she began to gather up the cups and saucers and cake plates, stacking them together. She carried them to the sink, then turned, glancing at her wrist watch. She grimaced.

"Anne, dear girl, I hate to impose on you, especially after my mother-hen speech just now. But so long as you are determined to be a slave to Metcalf's, could I persuade you to set up a small dinner party for me? This man called while you were out this morning and ordered dinner for two to be brought to his hotel suite. It's an easy menu, nothing elaborate. You don't have to do anything except leave it in the kitchen on war-mers where he can find it. He doesn't want the meal served, doesn't want a waitress hanging around in the way—you know the kind of thing?"

Anne had to smile at Iva's droll expression. She un-derstood perfectly. It was the sort of thing she could do with her eyes shut.

"I would carry it over, but Joe and I have tickets to a symphony this evening, and as soon as he comes in with the delivery van I've got to drag him home and get him into his best bib and tucker. You know how that is!"

"I'll be glad to do it," Anne said, and meant it. The more she had to do, the less time she would have to think. The more exhausted she was, the more likely she would be to sleep.

The number of the hotel room Iva had given her proved to be a penthouse suite high above the city in one of Dallas's most luxurious hotels. A uniformed por-ter rode with her and her wheeled cart laden with covered dishes up in the service elevator to the top floor. He waited politely while she rang the bell. No one answered. Under the disapproving eye of her es-cort, she used the key that had been provided for just such a contingency. As she wheeled her cart in through the open door, the elevator doors slid silently to behind her, and she was alone in the penthouse.

The kitchen was well equipped, a modern laboratory of stainless steel and chrome, with gleaming yellow surfaces and warm touches of wood paneling. Beside an array of the usual electrical appliances there was a large, glass-topped warming tray and a compact microwave oven. She could either place the food she had brought on the warmer to keep it an even temperature, or leave it to be quickly heated by micro-waves.

Anne unloaded the cart and pushed it into the corner. The food was packed in a series of plastic foam boxes to seal in either heat or cold and prevent spillage.

Her movements were swift but sure. She had to hurry. If the customer objected to a waiter, he would not be at all pleased to find her there when he returned. The first box she opened with perfect precision, and then her fingers grew clumsy and uncoordinated as one by one the others revealed their contents.

Trout marguery, asparagus in butter, French bread; fresh, ripe pears, chilled white wine . . .

It was the menu Ramón had requested weeks before, complete to the last detail. The menu she had delivered to his plane on that disastrous day when they had first met.

A stricken look in her eyes, Anne gripped the cabinet, staring at the food spread out before her. She was being foolish, she tried to tell herself. It was only a coincidence. It did not help. The pain within her heart grew boundlessly, spreading like poison throughout her body.

At the sound of a quiet footfall behind her, her ragged nerves jumped uncontrollably. She whirled, her eyes wide, her face pale with dread.

Ramón stood in the doorway.

"Good evening," he said, his voice level, his gaze pinioning her where she stood. "Could I persuade you to share my dinner, my dearest Anne?"

Weakness flooded over her. If the cabinet had not been behind her she would have fallen. As it was she reached back with both hands, pressing the open palms against it for support. The color receded from her face, leaving it the color of the white chunky sweater she wore over slim-fitting navy pants beneath her pea jacket.

Ramón had had longer to get used to her presence. His face mirrored no surprise at seeing her there. It crossed her mind to wonder, however, if he had been ill. He was thinner and there were lines carved into his face that she did not remember. He too wore a sweater with dark dress pants. Of earthy terra-cotta, it emphasized the lean grace of his tall frame.

"Well?" he queried softly. "Have you nothing to say to my invitation?"

It was an effort to force words through the constriction in her throat. "No, I . . . couldn't think of intruding."

"Intruding?" He lifted an eyebrow. "On what?"

"You—you did order dinner for two, didn't you? I'll be out of your way in a minute." Unconsciously Anne was listening, straining to hear the shrill sound of Irene's voice. At any second she expected the woman to appear, smiling in malicious triumph.

"If you go, I will have to eat alone. You are my only guest."

At the back of Anne's mind dawned the slow realization that Iva had known that Ramón would be here waiting for her—that Iva had deliberately omitted to give her his name.

"How did you manage this? What did you tell Iva to make her agree to it?"

"You are thinking of the threat I made once to

withdraw my business if they did not concur with my wishes, I think," he said shrewdly. "There was nothing like that. When I spoke to your employer's wife on the phone this morning, I told her the exact truth. At first she was reluctant either to tell me where you lived or to give you a message asking you to meet me somewhere. Later, when I called again she told me what she had planned. I made no objection. In fact, I was overjoyed."

"Why?" she asked, anger at the betrayal lending strength to her voice. "What do you want?"

"There are a few matters which need clearing up between us. The first of them is this."

He took out his wallet and from it extracted a slip of paper which he placed in Anne's hand.

She accepted it automatically, glancing down at it. The figures on it wavered and became distinct. It was a check for a phenomenal amount of money made out to herself.

"What is this?" she asked blankly.

"It is the salary we agreed upon, payment in full for two weeks labor in the role of my fiancée. Your acceptance of this money will dissolve all bonds between us and cancel any further obligation."

His businesslike tone repelled her. Without hesitation, Anne thrust the check back at him. "It's too much," she said, her voice sharp.

He made no move to accept it. A diabolical glint came into his eye. "Am I to take it, then, that you have no wish to see an official end to our engagement?"

"No!" Anne said, jerking her hand back.

"I thought not," he replied with grim satisfaction.

"Still, I can't take this much money," Anne told him, her tone as firm as she could make it.

"Why not? You've given back everything else I gave you."

"This is different."

"Why? Why is it different so long as I want you to have it?"

It was useless to argue. Anne let her arm fall to her side. Very well, she told herself with a mutinous set to her mouth. She would keep the piece of paper bearing his signature as a momento. She did not have to cash it.

"There is also the matter of a piece of luggage sent to you in Mexico by Iva Metcalf. Abuelita took possession of it when it arrived, it seems, and only yesterday 'remembered' where she had directed it to be stored. She meant no harm, only an excuse to allow herself the pleasure of outfitting you as she would any young relative."

Anne was not surprised. She had suspected a deception of some kind when she discovered from Iva that the suitcase had, in fact, been shipped. But she did not see the piece sitting about, and she had no intention of waiting until it was brought out.

"I am afraid I will have to trouble you to have it delivered to my apartment," she said, and could not resist adding as she moved toward the door, "I'm sure you will find it easy to persuade Iva to give you the address. Now if that is all . . ."

His arm shot out, blocking her passage. "That isn't all," he grated, allowing his irritation at her defensive attitude to color his tone.

"I fail to see what else there can be," Anne said and, with a quick twist of her body, ducked under his arm.

She was halfway to the door when a hand on her shoulder spun her around. A hard forearm caught her under the knees and she felt herself swung up against the unyielding planes of Ramón's chest. He carried her the few steps to a gold velvet sofa, where he dropped her on the soft cushions and then sat down beside her.

She sat up, a tinge of furious color in her cheeks.

Before she could swing her feet to the floor, he leaned over her, pinning her in one corner.

Unsmiling, he drawled, "I thought we could discuss the situation in a civil fashion over dinner, but if you won't have that, we can do it this way."

Anne's heart was thudding against her ribs. She was disturbingly aware of his nearness and her helpless position.

"The—the food will get cold," she protested in a small voice.

"To hell with the food. I want to talk to you, and we are going to talk if I have to tie you down to make you listen!"

Anne pressed her lips together, raising her chin. "You could have spoken to me at any time during this past two weeks. I fail to see the reason for your impatience now."

"Do you?" he said grimly. "Then perhaps I can enlighten you. But first, you have not inquired after my grandmother's health. Tell me, why is that?"

A pang of fear lent a quaver to Anne's voice. "Has something happened. Is Doña Isabel ill?"

"No," he answered with menacing slowness. "Nothing has happened. Abuelita is enjoying her usual robust health, just as she has ever since the day you left. But I only discovered that fact yesterday when I threatened to bring in a specialist to examine her. You, however, according to Abuelita, knew her secret before you left two interminable, unendurable weeks ago."

Anne, taken aback, thought she saw the reason for the hint of suffering in his choice of words. "I'm sorry you were anxious about her," she said defensively, "but I could hardly come bearing tales to you about your grandmother."

"No, of course not," he replied with a fierce gesture, as though he would push her attempt to explain from him. "Don't apologize! It is I who should apologize for being so blind. I should have known you would not have run away and left Abuelita when she needed you most. I should have realized you would not have disappeared without a word to anyone unless you had a good reason."

The air left Anne's lungs as if she had been struck a blow to the heart. She could not bring herself to meet the raking probe of Ramón's eyes. "It's all right," she said, in a tone heavy with finality.

If he noticed the hint that she would like to consider the subject closed, he ignored it, making no move to let her up from the sofa. Instead, he reached to slip his fingers around her neck, beneath her hair, rubbing the angle of her jaw with his thumb in a gentle caress.

"I can't help wondering," he went on as though she had not spoken, "exactly why you did leave. What was it that made you bolt like a frightened rabbit? Was it Irene? Or was it—me?"

Anne flicked a glance at the stillness that had closed over his features, then looked away again. What could she answer that would not betray herself? She could think of nothing. She could not think at all. The gentle movement of his thumb sent shivers of pleasure along her nerves and she grew minutely more aware of an aching need to move into his arms and press herself against him.

His grip became firmer, more insistent. "Look into my eyes, Anne, *mi alma*, and tell me I did not frighten you with my jealous temper."

Startled, Anne lifted her lashes. "Jealous?" she repeated.

"Of course," he replied, a rough edge creeping into his voice. "Insanely, wildly jealous. Don't you know yet that I love you more than life itself, and that you are mine and I cannot tamely stand by and watch any man put his hands on you. My anger then, *querida*, was not only that Pépé dared to touch you, but that you could not see that you belonged to me, only to me."

"You—you love me?" Anne asked, returning with a sense of awe to the most important point.

"Ah, mi vida, more than life itself," he answered, his voice husky in his throat, his accent becoming more pronounced.

Disbelief still clouded her eyes. "I thought you distrusted me, that you detested the kind of woman you thought I was."

"I tried, but what could I do? Even if you were the most avaricious witch alive, I had to have you near me. Why else would I hire a fiancée? Am I not man enough to rid myself of a clinging leech like Irene and protect my name from her vicious tongue without resorting to such schemes?"

She should have realized the truth of that assertion long before. Hadn't she seen evidence enough of the implacable strength of his will?

"Then you didn't need me, or my help, at all?" she asked in slow comprehension.

Before the words had left her mouth his arms closed around her. They were anything but gentle. The fierceness of his ardor swept over her like a raging fire. He kissed her eyelids, her forehead, her earlobes, trailing fire across her cheek to scorch her lips. She was crushed against him as he foiled any attempt at escape, even if she wished to try. She did not. The certainty of his love spread like healing balm to every corner of her mind. Beneath it her own desire kindled to flame so that her arms stole around his neck and she molded herself to the hard strength of his body.

With a deep, trembling breath, he released his hold. She lay back in his arms pent and breathless. After a moment, he shook his head.

"Why? Why did you run away when I tried before

to tell you how much I wanted you, how much I needed you?"

A deeper shade of color flushed Anne's cheeks. He had just declared their engagement officially null and void. How could she say to him that on that other occasion he had mentioned neither love nor marriage when even now, with words of love on his lips, he had not offered her his name. Still, she had to say something.

"I—I was afraid."

"You were afraid I intended to possess you without vows of marriage being said between us, were you not? But if that is so, why did you later leave my house rather than agree to be my wife as Abuelita wished?"

The bewildered humility of the question was totally out of character. It hurt her to see him so uncertain. Lifting her eyes, she met his questioning black gaze without evasion. "Because there was no mention of the word love in that marriage arranged by your grandmother, and I could not stand the torture of loving with all my heart a husband who cared nothing for me in return."

"Querida . . ." he whispered, drawing her close against him, nestling her head in the curve of his neck. "So you do love me."

"Yes," she murmured. "So much I can't tell you."

He sighed. "My stupid pride. When I think of the time we have wasted I cannot forgive myself. How can I ask you to forgive me?"

"No, no," she whispered incoherently, and lifted her lips to his in the age-old benediction, absolving him with a kiss.

Sometime later, Anne stirred. "You are certain Doña Isabel is well?" she asked. As he gave his assent, he went on. "And you are not still angry with her for deceiving you?"

Ramón stretched in lazy relaxation, running his

hand along her arm, and with the movement pushing up the sleeve of her sweater so he could press his lips to the soft skin at the turn of her elbow.

"How can I be?" he asked, his breath warm against her skin as he spoke without lifting his head. "It was she who gave me the first indication that under your cool disdain you were not indifferent to me."

Remembering her admission of love to his grandmother, Anne smiled, touching her fingers to the crisp waves of his hair.

Abruptly Ramón raised his head; pushing her sleeve higher, he examined the skin of her forearm. "These bruises," he said, a black scowl drawing his heavy brows together. "I made them . . . ?"

She had no choice but to admit it.

With a groan, he brushed the yellowish-purple discolored skin of the old bruise with his lips, then drew her close.

"I don't wonder that you fled from me," he breathed, kissing the soft wave of her hair at her temple in an agony of remorse. "But I would never willingly harm you, you know that."

Happily, Anne nodded.

"Then promise me, my heart, that you will never leave me again?"

Anne drew back, searching his face, her eyes radiant with the glow of love. "Never," she answered, her voice soft yet firm, "Never in this life—or afterward."